GODS AND CHILDREN

BOOK I

AIN'T NO MOUNTAIN

JANET TAYLOR-PERRY

Ain't No Mountain

Janet Taylor-Perry

Book 1
Gods and Children

Dragon Breath Press
Ridgeland, MS
http://www.dragonbreathpress.com/

ISBN: 978-0-9990692-7-1

OTHER BOOKS BY JANET TAYLOR-PERRY

The Raiford Chronicles:

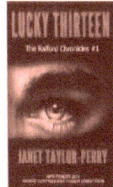   

Lucky Thirteen
http://amzn.to/1ld8grm
Heartless
http://amzn.to/1iWuYmP
Broken
http://goo.gl/6YTwyz
Whatever It Takes
http://goo.gl/1eLv66
The Legend of Draconis:

King Satin's Realm
http://goo.gl/wf7UbM
Spirits' Desire
Winner: Preditors and Editors Award
2017, Best "Other" Novel
goo.gl/H9St2K

April Chastain Intrigues:

Wilted Magnolias
https://goo.gl/2oJOjc

Hillbilly Hijinks

Homegrown Healer
https://www.amazon.com/dp/0999069233

Laura Beth Copeland Misadventures

Head Count
https://amzn.to/2msMt9z

AIN'T NO MOUNTAIN

DISCLAIMER

THE following is a complete work of fiction. Any resemblance to any person, living or dead, or any place is coincidence, and you, as a reader, have more vivid imagination that I do.

ACKNOWLEDGEMENTS

I must as always thank my editor, friend, and mentor, Lottie Boggan.

Great appreciation to many fellow authors who continually offer me encouragement: Melanie, Patricia, Terry, Glen, Darden, Philip, John F., Dot, Marty, Mike, Joss, Leslie, Apryl, Gemma, Susan M., Jeanne, Cathy, Sol, Rebecca, Hazel, Reni, Gerald, Reva, James, Vivian, Judy, Wynne, Mary, Carlene, Graeme, Rhiannon, Dena, Tammy, Bill, Randall, Linda, John R., Patti, David, Susan S., Forest, Melissa, Jazmine, Mark, Janet F., Johnny, Carole, Janice, Charna, Lydia, Edrie, CC, Luna, Patricia N-D., Malcolm, Michael, Chuck G., Chuck M., Ann, Dirk, T Cat, DelSheree, NancyKay, Charlotte, Bonnie, Robert, Meagan, Christopher, Dorian, Elizabeth. Please forgive me if I've forgotten anyone.

A special tribute goes to The Red Dog Writers for listening to this story in its earliest form, even if a few of them might have been shocked by my interpretation of Nephilim.

A shout out must go to my loyal fan and dear friend and beta reader, Nidia Hernandez, aka Barbra Best, author of *The Rock Star Records*. Also, thanks to a former student and beta reader, Gracie Hamby, who read this before its very first edit.

I must give praise to my family for their support, even when I snap their heads off because they interrupt my muse.

As always, the highest praise goes to Christopher Chambers (juroddesigns.com) for another outstanding cover design.

Also, I cannot express how valuable my proofreaders are—but if there are still errors, it's their fault. 😊

And last, but definitely not least, I praise my Lord and Savior Jesus Christ for bestowing upon me the gift of painting with words.

DEDICATION

FOR MCat (Mary Catherine Perry), my only daughter who said she wanted her own book. This is it. Her escapades with two friends planted the seed for an adventure with triplets.

[5] The devil led him up to a high place and showed him in an instant all the kingdoms of the world. [6] And he said to him, "I will give you all their authority and splendor; it has been given to me, and I can give it to anyone I want to. [7] If you worship me, it will all be yours."

[8] Jesus answered, "It is written: 'Worship the Lord your God and serve him only.'"

Luke 4: 5-8

TABLE OF CONTENTS

NAMES (HUMANOID)

ALL BOOKS:

> Tornabolt, pronounced TORN-uh-bolt (Tor) Ignis—Wind/Weather Elemental
>
> Taekeyla, pronounced tequila (Tae, pronounced tay) Ignis—Water Elemental
>
> Terkoyze, pronounced turquoise (Terk) Ignis—Terra-Firma Elemental
>
> Illuminet Ignis—Mother of the triplets, Fire Elemental, Angel
>
> Yarwhin Ignis—Father of the triplets, Nephilim, Ultimate Protagonist
>
> Sabita Ignis—Lesser goddess, Great-grandmother of the triplets
>
> Fuascailt, pronounced foo-SCAILT Ignis—Leviaddan's daughter, Tor's to-be mate, Part Wulfgar
>
> Iontus Ignis—Fuascailt's son, a Seer
>
> Leviaddan, pronounced Levee-add-den, Ignis—Nephilim, Yarwhin's half-brother, Ultimate Antagonist

AIN'T NO MOUNTAIN:

> Salmyr Ignis—The beginning of trouble, Father of Yarwhin & Leviaddan
>
> Fayla Norotor—Leviaddan's mother
>
> Melita Kalt—Yarwhin's first wife

Chriostalach, pronounced KRI-oh-stŏ-lŏch Bŏgin—Winter Elf, Guardian of Örnland

Veelar Ignis—Orc, Leviaddan's offspring

Neeshawn Ignis—Veelar's mate, Orc

Creenon—Son of Veelar & Neeshawn, Infant Orc

CREATURES—*AIN'T NO MOUNTAIN*

YARWHIN'S ALLIES:

Evolved Danooks

Winter Elves

Iolar Mór Bán—Sentient, The Great White Eagle, Queen

Yeti—Goliab, Leader

Dryads—Tree Spirits, Yggamay & Yggadon

Caitheamh, pronounced CATH-um, Tobar (Toby)—Size-changing Raven, Sentient

Prince Rhagclaw—Iolar Mór Bán's son, Abducted, Heir to the Eagle throne

Evolved Orcs

Quill—Iolar Mór Bán's living feather

Rí Nal Tolair—dead Eagle King

LEVIADDAN'S MINIONS:

Simple Danooks

Drows

Banshees

Trolls

Gargoyles
Ice Warriors
Simple Orcs
Rhiamas

PLACES—*AIN'T NO MOUNTAIN:*

Salmyra—Post-apocalyptic world
Lumenesca—Fabled city
Libretante—Old library
Obsid—Hell
Pearlan—Heaven
Sáru Saoil Cuardaign Anan, pronounced SŎ-Roo SAY-oil QUAR-dane A-non—Purgatory, Yarwhin's Obsidian Prison
Sliabh Aer, pronounced SLEE-ob AIR—Iolar Mór Bán's mountain nest
Örnland—An ice world
Lavan—A fire world; its residents are called Lavanians
Carrion Tuirlingthe, pronounced TOUR-length—Plain at the entrance to Örnland
Conflatile Montem—Volcano where the Fire Brazier of Lavan was hidden
Reoite, pronounced RAY-it, Tundra, Theas, pronounced TAY-us—The southernmost part of Salmyra where Yarwhin's first wife lived

ANIMALS—*AIN'T NO MOUNTAIN:*

Fiery Termant—army ant-termite cross
Doose—duck-goose cross
Horsenae—equines
Lellepant—pachyderms
Camalia—camels
Clucks-chickens
Rhiamas-skeletal, flesh-eating fish
Tiggra—tiger

1
GODS OR CHILDREN?

DEATH. Decay. Destruction. This is all the three people who topped the hill had ever known.

Salmyra was a world in ruin. For centuries the factions fought, until they all but destroyed one another.

Still, they fought. They fought for food. They fought for fire. They fought for fun. But none fought for or with honor.

Those who did not fight, traveled. They were constantly on the move, searching. Though the daytime sirocco scorched exposed skin, the nomads dared not move at night on their quest to find the fabled city of Lumenesca. They dared not brave the darkness when the winds stopped blowing and the cloud of dust no longer swirled in the sirocco but settled into a low-lying blanket that shrouded the land in death. No one journeyed at night for fear of falling prey to the Danooks, those rumored to have survived the flesh-melting weapons used in the final battle. Now, they could not tolerate the faintest light and desired man-flesh for nourishment—and legend told that woman-flesh was even tastier to them.

The three on the hill had once trekked across the world with their mother searching for answers. After a decade, she had finally found what she sought, and they had stopped. The past three years, they had been in one place. She called it Libretante.

Thirteen-year-old Tornabolt stretched his lean, wiry body and turned his head side to side. His granite-gray eyes caught his sisters', Taekeyla having aqua-marine irises and Terkoyze with deepest brown, as the wind stopped whipping his long chestnut tresses around his face.

"The nomads should be stopping shortly." He pointed at the sojourners. Each dressed in drab earth-tones and covered themselves from head to foot, with thin layers of gauzy material over their faces to protect skin and eyes from cutting sand grains. They pulled pop-bubbles from packs on their backs and set up camp where they halted. Each group rolled strands of heavy twine, barbed at intervals with bone shards, glass, sharp stones, or metal, as could be found, around the perimeter of their faction. The color of the pop-bubbles denoted which ideology they supported.

To Tornabolt's right, Taekeyla laid a hand on his arm. The wind had all but died, and the dust cloud began its descent, causing her long silvery-blonde hair to hang limp. "Mamere told us not to wander far, just close enough to watch the nomads."

Tornabolt's and Taekeyla's triplet and identical to her sister in appearance, except her eye color, Terkoyze said, "We should get back."

The girls' lithe bodies seemed to float as they turned around. Their tan gauzy skirts that had lashed around their muscular legs only moments before draped over rounding hips of developing womanhood.

In loose beige breeches, shirt, and vest, Tornabolt followed a step behind.

***

The siblings picked up their pace as grunting and snarling caught their ears. "Danooks!" said Tornabolt, pointing out two large human-like figures emerging from a clump of cacti surrounded by sagebrush. The creatures' large eyes and somewhat pointed noses and mouths gave their faces a distinctive dog-like countenance.

Frantic trills from the nomads not yet fully camped spurred the teens into a full-out run. The two Danooks they had spotted had caught their scent and pursued them in hopes of fresh, tender flesh.

Loud wailing accompanied the triplets as they closed the heavy wooden door of the partially-razed building they called home. Although out of breath, a pleasant aroma took their minds off their near escape of the Danooks' waking.

Illuminet Ignis turned from lighting the single tallow with its wick of twisted animal gut. "You three cut that too close."

"We're all right, Mamere," Tornabolt said with a reassuring smile. "What's for supper?"

"Roasted boar shoulder with mushrooms and onions. I shot a large one today. I'm salting the rest." She popped him playfully on the head with the fleece mitt she held. "Don't try to change the subject, Tor. I didn't walk all those leagues with ropes around my waist tethered to your arms in order to keep you near me so that we could find this place for you to be so careless. Don't risk your lives again."

"Mamere," Terkoyze said, "how can you be sure this is the place you sought? More than half of it is crumbled in ruins."

"The scrolls, Terk." Illuminet waved a hand around them. Cubbyhole after cubbyhole was filled with scrolls.

Taekeyla rolled her eyes. "Which you read every day and make us read every day."

"You three are special, Tae. Soon you'll come into your powers and here is where you'll learn to control them."

"We know, Mamere," said Tor in a placating manner. "We are supposedly the Elemental Gods reborn."

Terk added, "Mamere, you do realize that any folk we journey with think you're crazy.

Nobody believes in gods anymore. Look at this world. What kind of gods let this happen?"

"The kind that was usurped!" Illuminet snapped. "Soon when your powers manifest, you'll understand. Then, you can help your father."

The triplets looked from one to another. They had never known their father. They were unsure if Illuminet knew who he was. She had always insisted he was of some great importance. More likely, according to anyone who knew her, she had either been seduced or given herself to a member of a warring faction to stay alive. She had conceived, and in an attempt to maintain some form of sanity and make the children she bore feel wanted, she made up a story. But they had always felt loved.

Tornabolt, the one who resembled his mother most in appearance, but only in facial features, asked softly as his mother served plates and passed them out, "Mamere, who is he? Do you know?"

"Yes, but I cannot tell you. I am forbidden until your powers appear."

Terkoyze snorted. "Yes. We've heard a thousand times. Tor will be able to control the wind and weather. Tae will bring forth life-giving liquid. And I will bless the terra-firma— but only *if* we succeed in helping free this *father* that has never once laid eyes on us."

"Stop it!" Tor rebuked his sister. "You will not speak to Mamere with such disrespect."

She hissed and turned away from her brother.

Taekeyla asked, "Mamere, if we are these three Elementals, where is Fire?"

Illuminet sighed. "First, children, I was not seduced or raped as many say. I was chosen." She rolled her hand with her fingers in a wave-like motion until the top of her hand was on the bottom and her palm made a small cup. A tiny ball of fire flickered to life, but it did not burn her. "I am Fire—and Light. But that's all I can tell you." Amber eyes glowed a momentary red, and lava-like locks fell over her shoulders as Illuminet bowed her head. "My power will not be full-strength until..." She trailed off and dipped a piece of unleavened bread in the juice of the boar. She chewed slowly and swallowed. "And your father *has* seen you. Eat and rest. Tomorrow I need to send you to another sector. You will need to camp, and I cannot go with you this time."

"Where are we going, Mamere?" Tor asked.

"To your father. But you will need to follow the map I'll have for you to the letter. The Mound of the Obelisk is your goal."

They ate in silence.

The meal finished, Illuminet cleaned up while the triplets prepared for bed and a trek the next day. She came to each one's mat to kiss their foreheads.

"I'm sorry, Mamere," Terk said.

"All is forgiven. Sleep, my children."

She snuffed the tallow and lay on her own mat. *Sleep. Dream. For after tomorrow, I might never see you again.*

2
ABYSS

MORNING brought a somber breakfast with very little conversation. Illuminet double-checked the packs from the night before. One pop-bubble for the three teens fit into Tae's backpack. Tor got the privilege of carrying the coiled barbed twine, and Terk's pack held a scroll and map. "Follow this without detour," warned their mother.

Each child's pack contained one change of clothes, a pouch each of unleavened bread, dried fruit, and jerky, along with several skins of brown water and juice drawn from the numerous prickly cacti in the terrain. All three knew how to get more juice should they need it and which berries and wild plants were edible.

In addition to food, beverage, and clothing, each child carried flint and stone, as well as weapons. Each had a dagger on a sheath hanging from a leather thong belt around their waists and a long-range weapon. Terk carried a sling and a pouch with several smooth stones. Tae had her bow and a full quiver of arrows while Tor carried both a javelin and a long sword.

With each of her children outfitted for a journey, Illuminet kissed them on the cheek as tears streamed down hers. The hiss as her tears hit the ground confirmed her assertion that she was "Fire." Small streams of steam rose, creating a fine mist. "I will be right here waiting for you," she choked. "I love you."

In turn, each child hugged their mother and exited the safety of the old, partially destroyed library.

***

The triplets fell into step behind a group of travelers. When the nomads stopped, they stopped with them. The first night gave them their first obstacle.

Tae unrolled their pop-bubble. Each sibling took an edge. With a lift and quick snap, their temporary shelter of tightly woven hemp canvas over prepared animal skin gave a loud *POP*! A dome shot up. Fast-placed stakes of whatever long, sharp material could be found, completed the setup. The triplets were lucky enough to have stakes of metal that had been found along the way during the years they had traveled with Illuminet.

Amid orange, blue, brown, and gray pop-bubbles, theirs was white, the fur of tundra bear having been used. The children recalled moving from a cold climate to the sweltering area they now traversed.

A man rolling rope around the camp of orange—Fire supporters—growled, "No loyalty to anything."

Thinking, *dye for animal skins is more important to you than using your resources to protect your family*, Tor replied, "We adhere to truth and unity."

The man started toward the lad, and Tae nocked an arrow. "I don't miss," she hissed.

With the dust cloud quickly descending, the man backed away and finished camp.

The teens escaped to the privacy of their pop-bubble. Their meal meager, they turned in early and waited for dawn through a tentative slumber.

Howling jerked all three awake. They peeked from the opening of their pop-bubble. Just beyond the most distant shelter, they made out snouted, humanoid figures circling the camp and stopping periodically to bay at the obscured half-orb of a moon.

The triplets watched as the Danooks tested the barbed twine fences, jumping back each time one was pricked.

Tor sighed and closed the opening, his heart pounding with the reality that struck him. When they sat close together, he whispered, "I don't remember them trying so hard to get through. Soon they'll figure out how to separate the strands, and we will not be safe without stronger shelter."

"Then we should determine a better way to camp," Tae asserted.

"Above ground—maybe in tree branches," Terk said.

"Most trees are off any road," their brother pointed out.

Terk nodded. "True. But according to the map, we'll soon branch off from any well-worn path."

"Then tomorrow, we diverge from the crowd," Tor said. "Now, let's rest while we can."

***

Travel in the rising heat the next day made conversation a chore. They made sure to stay far back from the man who had challenged them the night before.

Tae, a few steps behind her siblings stopped. They turned as she nocked an arrow. With a nod, she indicated her target—a hare. Her mark was true, and she scampered to retrieve supper, dropping the animal into her pack.

The journey continued with only short stops for drink and a quick bite of jerky or fruit. A good hour before the nomads they trailed would make camp, Terk placed a hand on each of her siblings' chests. "Look." She tipped her head to a rise off to the side of the trail. "A cave. Let's check it out."

"What if that's where the Danooks sleep?" asked Tor barely above a whisper.

"I guess we kill them in their slumber," Terk replied without pause and pulled out her dagger.

Tae followed her example, and Tor drew his long sword.

The three crept to the opening. Picking a bit of dried grass from the slope, Tae used her flint and stone to start a small fire balanced on the flat of her weapon. It was just enough to give illumination for a few feet. She thrust her hand into the mouth of the cave. The flame flickered on the walls.

"Empty," she breathed with relief and walked into the cave, not much larger than the pop-bubble would be when set up. She advanced to the center and grunted. "Looks like someone before had this idea. There's a fire pit with kindling. Bring more twigs."

Soon she had a fire going and took the rabbit from her pack to skin. "I'll cook. Fortify the opening with the twine and cover it with thatch, but be quick."

Tor and Terk hastily created a weave of twigs and grass and placed it over the opening behind them as they stepped inside. Terk felt the wall around the entrance. "Tae was right. There are pegs here for the rope."

In only a few minutes, they had a zigzag and crisscross of barbed twine behind the woven branches and grass.

A distant rumble brought a smile to Tor's lips. "I wished for rain." He wiggled eyebrows toward his sisters. "Maybe my powers are manifesting."

Terk punched his arm. "No matter, Tor. It will give us added protection tonight."

As they ate the rabbit cooked over the campfire, torrential rain began to pelt the ground. It fell faster, and hail joined the large raindrops. Water crept into the cave.

"For the sake of the gods!" shrieked Terk. "Tor, if you caused this, make it stop. We'll drown in here."

"I don't know how!" the boy yelled back at his sister.

"Take my hands!" Tae ordered, thrusting a hand at each sibling.

They grasped hands. "Now try," she said to Tor without anger.

"Stop…stop…stop," Tor chanted.

Wind gusted. Lightning flashed. Then, a fine drizzle set in.

"You did it," said Tae, giving her brother a hug. Then, she grabbed a couple of empty water skins and stuck them outside the cave entrance.

"By the gods!" Terk said, staring at her brother.

Tor shook his head. "If I *did* start the storm, I have no control. I only wished for rain." He exhaled long and loud. "Let's sleep. I'm exhausted."

The triplets tried to sleep, but they were jolted awake by howling and then screaming.

Tor let out a long, shuddering breath. "I dread to think what we'll find in the morning."

"That will be another day." Terk shrugged when her brother and sister eyed her.

"Not cold," she said. "Practical. We need to rest and worry about another day with the sunrise."

Tae took both their hands. "Let's scoot to the very back of the cave and stay close together."

***

A new day and a mile's travel confirmed the fear of what had occurred in the night. Pop-bubbles of the nomads were tossed about; the barbed twine was bent and snapped; and multiple trails of blood led in many directions.

The rain that had fallen in the night before, had stopped within feet of the camp, but flasks Tae positioned outside the cave where the triplets slept, had been filled with clean water.

The three now looked around them. "Thank the gods we stopped," said Terk.

"Thought you didn't believe in gods," Tor taunted his sister.

"Well, maybe your powers, Mr. Weather-maker, did come to fruition last night and saved us."

"I hope Mamare got rain, too," Tae said with a catch in her voice. "But not the storm."

"We'll be back with her soon," assured Tor with a hand to her shoulder.

Terk looked around again. "There's nothing we can do here. We need to move on." She pulled the map from her pack. "This indicates the rugged path is about half a day away." She pointed out the direction. "This shows a wooded area. We'll have to test the in-the-trees theory tonight. Let's move."

Tor pointed to the mayhem. "We just leave this?"

"Yes," asserted Tae. "It'll serve as warning to any other travelers that the Danooks have evolved."

"No longer mindless beasts looking for a meal. Now thinking predators." Tor pushed his long brown hair back and tied it with a leather thong.

"Yes." Tae took her brother's hand. "Let's go."

The wind blew mercilessly, grains of sand biting into exposed skin. Before long, all three wore ponytails and had covered their faces with gauze scarves. Still, they had to shield their eyes with their gauze-gloved hands.

They trudged down the dusty road for several hours before stopping to rest and eat, taking shelter from the wind behind a humongous fiery termant mound. Tor reminded his sisters, "Be careful not to touch the mound. Those bugs can strip our skin from us in seconds." Skeletal remains of animals around the mound confirmed his assessment.

Terk took out the map again. "Only a mile more or just over." Trees had begun to cluster in small bunches, but a shade indicated something larger ahead. "Keep a sharp lookout." She rubbed her gritty, grimy arm. "Hey, if Tor actually conjured up that rain, Tae, how about getting us a brook for bathing?"

Tae rolled her eyes. "If it *was* our brother, it's not sorcery. It's the power of a god."

Terk snorted a laugh.

Tae commenced to draw in the dirt, little snake-like lines. Deeper she dug with her finger while her brother and sister watched. Water began to bubble. Tae clapped gleefully and jumped over the water to point triumphantly at Terk and Tor.

Suddenly, water burst from the ground in triple geysers, thrusting the three off the path with force.

"Tae, not exactly what I meant!" yelled Terk.

"Sorry!" Tae hollered over the roar of the water from the other side of the path from her siblings.

Tor grabbed Terk's hand and reached through the churning water to grasp Tae's hand. "Just like I did!" he shouted. "Think about making it smaller. None of us have control. It takes all of us."

Tae kept saying, "Just a brook."

After ten minutes, the geysers became springs. "They won't last long," said Tae. "Take your choice. Bathe and wash the clothes you wear."

Another fifteen minutes and the springs subsided to a trickle, but a rivulet of water formed. Tae smiled. "Years from now, this will be a brook."

"By the gods!" Terk looked at her hand. "Is it true? Are we?"

Tor grinned. "Seems Mamere spoke the truth."

"What can I do?" Terk began pointing at pebbles to make them move. She blew on the parched grass. "Nothing!" she screamed.

Tor took her hand. "Stop. Yesterday, I caused a *storm,* not a gentle rain as I wanted. Today, Tae began a brook, but almost killed us. You are third-born. Maybe tomorrow. Still, none of us can function without the others."

"Patience," Tae echoed.

"Fine!" Terk huffed. "Let's get going."

In clean clothes and feeling refreshed, the three continued their trek.

***

"Here!" Terkoyze shouted an hour later.

A trail off the main-traveled path was barely visible going into a patch of woodland, a sight seldom seen by the triplets. Terk pointed. "According to the scroll Mamere sent, we're to look for the Mound of the Obelisk. That's where we'll find our way to…"

"Our father," the other two finished her statement.

Tornabolt looked toward the setting sun. "But that will have to wait. We need to get into this"—He ran his hand down a tree trunk— "thicket. I've never seen so many trees together."

Terk stepped onto the nearly non-existent path. "If I'm the Terra-Firma goddess, this is my world!"

No more than a hundred feet in, they came to a massive oak, limbs large and low. Terk pointed skyward. "Up there. The pop-bubble will fit perfectly in that cluster of limbs."

"We can wrap the twine around the trunk as we go up," suggested Taekeyla.

"No!" snapped Terk. "The tree would protest the shards poking into its bark."

Tor suggested, "Let's coil it on the ground near the trunk. The Danooks will step on the spikes if they come this way. They'll yowl in pain."

"Good idea." Terk nodded. "Yggamay agrees."

"Who?" asked Tae.

"Our new friend." Terk patted the tree. It sounded as if the tree sighed.

Wire wrapped in seven concentric circles, the triplets scaled the trunk fifty feet into the air to a cluster of three long limbs. There, they pitched the pop-bubble, which fit snuggly against the trunk. Each limb provided a firm place to unroll a sleeping mat. They dined on the dried fruit, bread, and jerky before they slept soundly and safely.

***

Morning came with deep shadows. The triplets broke camp and descended Yggamay. They repacked the twine and discovered a mass of wild blackberries. Breakfast was sweet and juicy.

Tor extended his arm out, palm up. "Lead the way, Miss Goddess of the Terra-Firma."

"Ha, ha." But Terk took the lead.

"I believe the forest is getting thicker," whispered Tae an hour in. "I don't like all the shadows."

Tor took her hand and pulled her along as they followed Terk.

Tae continued to worry. "It's so dark in here the Danooks could be about."

"Sh," Tor warned. "The quieter the better."

"Too late!" yelled Terk as a large humanoid with elongated canines crashed through the undergrowth.

"Run!" Tor ordered, pulling out his long sword.

The girls raced toward an area ahead that looked brighter.

With one swift swing of the sword, the Danook's head left its shoulders, but three more creatures appeared on each side of the path from the darkness.

"By the gods!" bellowed Tor, and he took flight behind his sisters.

Far enough away to take a breath, Tae and Terk turned. Seeing their brother being pursued by half a dozen Danooks, Terk fitted a stone into her sling and Tae nocked a broadhead arrow rather than the dart-like projectiles she used for small game.

Both fired, taking down a foe. Another arrow and another stone felled two more Danooks.

"Run! Damn it! Run!" Tor screamed.

The girls took off just as low growling started behind them. They flew into a canyon filled with light down the center, but with overhangs, which allowed shade and cover for Danooks unnumbered. The outcroppings sheltered a steep slope.

"Underground! They live underground," Terk said standing back-to-back with her sister and the two of them rotating a full three hundred sixty degrees. The stench of rot assailed them, and the fetid pant of the Danooks almost took their breath away.

Tor made it to the light. "Great! Just great!" he barked, seeing the gauntlet of Danooks. "Stay in the light and keep moving."

They ran.

The ground beneath their feet became sandier.

They ran.

The ground beneath their feet became squishy with sucking sounds on their moccasin-covered feet.

They ran.

The ground beneath their feet became a bog.

They began to struggle to move, sinking to their knees in sticky muck. The canyon sides closed in. One misstep and a Danook could grab them and pull them into the deep trenches on each side.

Terk stopped.

Her siblings plowed into her back.

"Move!" Tor belted.

"Look!" Terk cried, pointing up. "There it is! The Mound of the Obelisk."

On the canyon rim atop a dozen cylindrical boulders, stood a gleaming white obelisk.

"How does that save us?" shrieked Tae as a Danook's fingertips grazed her.

Tor roared, "Terra-Firma Goddess! Seal them off!"

Terk stretched her arms out to her sides, hands up with palms flat toward each canyon wall. Danooks clawed at her hands.

At first, tiny pebbles trickled down the walls. Then some sand. Followed by a trembling.

The triplets froze, watching the boulders on which the obelisk stood begin to sway, fall, tumble down.

"Move! Move! Move!" Tor commanded as rocks peppered them.

Forcing feet free of the quagmire, they managed five, six, seven steps as the first boulder crashed where they had stood.

Whoosh!

The ground swallowed them.

***

As if emerging from the birth canal, one-by-one, Tornabolt, Taekeyla, Terkoyze popped free of the suffocating slide into an abyss of oblivion.

3
OBSIDIAN OPPRESSION

TOR opened his eyes. Total Darkness. Deafening silence. *I'm alive.* He strained his ears for any sign of his sisters and then held his breath. *Not my breathing.* He moved his hand across a slick surface.

A groan got the boy's attention. "Oh. Tor?"

"Tae!"

Tor sat up and felt himself—arms, legs, midsection. *Nothing broken.* "Tae, talk to me so I can find you. Are you hurt?"

"I don't think so."

"Is Terk near you?"

"I can't see a thing." Tae felt around. Her hand touched corn-silk hair and a sticky ooze. "Terk!"

Crawling in the pitch-black toward his sister's voice, Tor's hand landed on her foot.

Tae screamed.

"It's me," Tor said.

Tae felt her sister's head. "Terk. Wake up." A hint of panic in her voice, she said, "She's bleeding, Tor."

Tor inched to sit beside Tae. He opened her pack and rummaged in it until he found her flint and stone. "Do you have anything we can light?"

"Use a piece of my skirt. I don't care."

"That won't last long. Do you still have the rabbit entrails?"

"Wrapped in a piece of cheesecloth, but they aren't dried enough to make a good wick."

"Better than nothing."

Tor found the gummy remains of their supper a few nights before. Pulling his dagger from its sheath, he cut a bit of gut along with a piece of the cloth. Fumbling in the dark, he wrapped the intestine tight against his dagger blade with the cloth. Then he sparked the flint and stone until the crude candle flamed, offering weak light, stinking with the burning flesh.

As Tor worked, Terk moaned and stirred. "Ow." She put her hand to her head and tried to sit.

After only seconds, she started and scanned the dimly lit space. "Did any of the Danooks fall with us?"

"I don't think so," replied Tae.

"I don't see anything." Tor stood and made a circle. "Where are we?"

The cavern they fell into appeared to be slick-walled. No stalagmites or stalactites were present, but a long shadow indicated something like a hallway.

Tae tended her sister. She washed the doose egg on Terk's forehead with water from a flask. "The cut is small. You must have landed face down."

"I think I'm all right now." Terk smiled. "Mamere would ask if I cracked the ground."

"She's only teasing you," Tor said.

"I know, but I *am* stubborn."

Tor's makeshift light flickered and went out.

"I really don't like it so dark," said Tae. She held her hand at the end of her nose. "I can't even see my hand right in front of me."

A scraping sound from the direction that could be a corridor caused the triplets to huddle close together.

"Get your daggers ready," Tor said. "Be prepared to stab whatever it is."

***

A light danced shadows on the walls of the long, dark passageway as the triplets waited, certain they were about to die.

A human form loomed ahead of them; a large shadow cast on the wall. The three stood in unison.

"Maybe we should attack it," whispered Terk.

"If we rush into the unknown, we might be the dead ones," Tor argued. "Let it come to us."

A brazier hanging from a chain swung into the room. The triplets blinked as the radiance blinded them.

"By the gods!" a voice said. "You've come. But you're injured."

A massive man with long hair, streaked silvery-white and dark-brown, stepped toward them.

Each child held a dagger at the ready.

The man stopped. "Tornabolt Ignis. Taekeyla Ignis. Terkoyze Ignis. Illuminet has done well. You have nothing to fear from me."

"Who are you?" Tor demanded.

"I am called Yarwhin Ignis. I am your father."

***

It seemed time stood still. No one spoke. The light from the lantern flitted across the obsidian walls. Yarwhin smiled at his children. In the golden light, his sky-blue eyes squinted and crinkled around the edges with his smile.

"Our father?" asked Terk. She pointed up. "We almost died up there."

Yarwhin held the lantern aloft. "I am unsure how you got here, but that is solid rock up there."

"Exactly where is 'here'?" asked Terk

"My home for the last two centuries."

"It can't be," said Tor. "We fell through a hole. Some kind of quagmire dragged us down." The boy shook his head. "Two centuries? How old are you?"

"Much older than two centuries." He scratched his head. "Interesting. It would seem my brother is still about." Yarwhin pursed his lips. "And were you pursued by beasts?"

"Danooks," confirmed Tae.

"Ah, yes." Yarwhin nodded. "The poor devils left behind by my brother."

"Brother?" asked Tor.

"I have a long story."

"You could start by telling us why you never cared enough to visit us and why you left Mamere alone with us." Terk arched her eyebrow and winced.

"I had no choice. Please." Yarwhin indicated the long tunnel with his hand. "Come with me."

"Why should we trust you?" asked Tor.

"I'm your father."

"So, you say." Terk sheathed her dagger and folded her arms across her chest.

Tor nodded agreement. "You must admit you've said some strange things. Like your age and a brother and you had no choice but to desert us."

"You're correct, my son."

"He *is* our father," said Tae, sheathing her dagger and stepping forward. Tor caught her arm. "It's fine," she said and turned to Yarwhin. "Do you have food?"

"Yes, dear one. Follow me."

***

The triplets sat on black cushions and took in the abundance of the item. No other furnishings seemed to be about, nowhere else to sit, no table, no bed—just a multitude of ebony pillows. In sconces around the shiny black walls burned seven golden torches.

Yarwhin slid the top back on an outcropping and spoke. "Four bowls of venison stew and four cups of apple ale and barley bread."

The children listened intently, but they heard no response. Yet, within minutes, Yarwhin passed out the food and took a serving for himself.

"Where did this come from?" Tor asked, dipping bread into the stew and savoring a bite.

"I don't know. My physical needs are met, but I have no company." He glared at each wall. "This prison of obsidian is oppression at its *finest*. I am useless surrounded by the material."

Terk knitted her brow. "How can a god be a prisoner?"

Her father gave a sardonic chuckle. "Ah." He sipped his ale. "Eat your meal and rest. When you wake, I'll tell you a story of adventure, betrayal, and now that you're finally here— hope."

4
A DISTANT WORLD

PALLETS of the softest, yet firmest, pillows made for sound sleeping. No noises or threats woke the triplets.

After a time, Tae awoke first. She saw her father looking in the covered overhang. Barefoot on cool, smooth stone, she approached him.

"Good morning, dear one," Yarwhin said without turning. "Did you sleep well, Taekeyla?"

The girl stopped. She looked around her at the large room that had not changed from the time before. "How do you know it's morning? How did you know it was me?"

"I have an internal timekeeper. It has been about eight hours since you went to bed. I knew it was you because you give off a spiritual essence of trust. Your ability to manipulate water gives you a quiet confidence, but you are still tentative."

"I almost killed us with the force I couldn't control."

"Your Elemental is powerful. It can squelch Fire and pulverize Terra-Firma. A tiny trickle will eventually wear down a mountain. In time, you will learn to control it."

"What about Wind?"

"No, Water and Wind together are almost unstoppable."

"Is that why I feel more connected to Tor?"

"Tor?"

"Tornabolt."

"Ah. Yes, I believe it is. Tor? Very well, and would you prefer Tae as I heard your siblings call you?"

"Yes. And Terk."

"Then I shall try to remember."

She pointed. "What is that thing?"

"My provider." He held his hand out to her. "Come and see."

Tae stood beside Yarwhin and looked into the recess. She turned her head up to stare at the man who was well over a foot and a half taller than she was. "I see swirling fog."

"That is also what I see, but it is a lighter gray at daytime. What would you like for breakfast?"

"Eggs. We haven't had eggs for a very long time."

"You heard my daughter. Eggs for four and sausage and melon and warm, spiced berry juice."

Tor wandered up, rubbing sleep from his eyes. "I heard what you said to Tae."

"Good morning," Yarwhin said. "Breakfast will be ready soon."

"Why did my powers show first?" asked Tor.

"I think you know."

"Birth order?"

"Yes."

Terk walked up. "Why is Mamere not able to do much?"

"It is a long story."

"That you promised to tell." Terk frowned. "I heard what you said, too. Why am I weaker than these two?"

"Not weaker," Yarwhin said. "Think for a moment. You have the ability to heal and nurture, but you must stop being so angry and impatient. Yes, you can cause damage, but to build up is so much more desirable."

He retrieved the food Tae had asked for and passed out trays of obsidian.

"None of you are yet able to control what you can do. Tor can whisper a spring rain or soft breeze. He can also blow a tempest so powerful it can bring half a sea onto land. But once the flood recedes the water will leave the land, but maybe in disarray. Tae can make a babbling brook or cascading waterfall. That same moisture is needed to make your Yggamay thrive, Terk."

"How do you know about Yggamay?"

"I once had all your abilities until I was betrayed."

They all sat on cushions and ate. Terk thought hard. "All right. So, just what are you? I mean, you're huge. Will we grow as big? Mamere is tall. Are you—we—gods?"

"No."

"Then, I don't understand. How can we have such powers? Are you—we—immortal?"

"No."

"But you said you are over two hundred," Tor interjected.

"Longevity does not equal immortality."

"So, you can die?" Tae asked, suddenly feeling scared. She stared at her father, eyes welling with tears.

"I can, and I will—someday." Yarwhin patted Tae's hand. "But I cannot be killed by any except one of my own kind."

"And that is?" Terk stretched her hand out.

Tae laid her hand on Yarwhin's. "What are you? What are we?"

"Nephilim."

***

The look on the teens' faces confirmed what Yarwhin had thought—they had no clue what Nephilim were. *Illuminet has kept her promise.*

He gathered the dishes and put them in the overhang with the cover. He pointed to another recessed area. "A water closet. You may bathe and attend to personal needs. When you get back, I'll try to explain."

The triplets cleaned up and found Yarwhin in the room where they had fallen.

"What's wrong, Papere?" Tae asked.

Yarwhin whirled around. "What did you say, child?"

Tae's eyes grew wide. "I didn't mean…"

"Hmm." Yarwhin shook his head. "You just made me very happy. I didn't expect that address." He rubbed his square jaw, thumb on one side and four fingers on the other. "Papere? I never thought I would like that term, but I find that I do." He took a moment to look each child in the eye.

"What did you call your father?" asked Tor.

"Father. At least to his face. Behind his back, Monster."

The three children looked from one to the other.

Yarwhin pointed up. "I was trying to determine how you fell through and how to return you."

"You don't want us here?" Terk asked, dipping the corners of her mouth.

"I want to be with you very much, but not here in this prison." He nodded. "Yes, it is a prison."

Tae barely whispered, "Do you love Mamare?"

Yarwhin smiled and his eyes gleamed. "Illuminet is my Angel." He started back to the big room. "Come. I'll tell you my story."

***

Yarwhin served sweet cakes and cold milk. Once again, the triplets were amazed for they had never tasted anything so delicious, nor had they ever experienced cold milk. Yarwhin's heart broke at the expressions on their faces.

Swallowing his anger at his brother for causing his children to suffer—yea, for forcing him to begat children at all—he said huskily, "Where would you like me to start?"

"What's a Nephilim?" Tor asked around a bite.

"Well, that's almost the beginning." Yarwhin nodded. "Nephilim are the offspring of children of gods and humans."

"So—only part god?" asked Terk still giving a bit of skepticism in her voice.

"Close." Yarwhin spoke into the overhang that seemed to supply his needs. "Canvas and paints."

For a change, there came a gurgling sound.

"No, they are not for eating. They are for drawing."

The gurgle came again.

"I want to amuse myself."

A moment later, Yarwhin lifted out several canvases and numerous paint pallets and other artistic paraphernalia. He closed the recess.

Tae whispered, "You understood what that sound said, and you lied."

Yarwhin arched an eyebrow. "How do you know I lied?"

Tae shrugged.

"You are very intuitive to the spirit—like your mother."

Terk opened her mouth. Yarwhin held up a hand. "I will get to Illuminet."

He leaned a canvas against the wall and sat beside it. "Yes, I lied just in case the wrong person should discover your whereabouts. I think the best way to explain would be to show you by joining our minds, but the obsidian prevents me from doing so. Therefore, I'll draw pictures to help. I lied because I do not think my brother realizes his attempt to kill you sent you to me—yet."

Tor started to speak. Yarwhin shook his head. "I'll get to my brother in time, also. His name is Leviaddan. But the story starts a millennium ago.

"Our father is a child of a god. He came here to Salmyra from a place called Obsid, where this stone originates. He and some of his siblings and cousins went on adventures to a great many different worlds."

"Other worlds?" Terk arched an eyebrow, mimicking her father's earlier facial expression to perfection.

"Yes, my dear, other worlds. Salmyra is only one of thousands. I have never been to any others, but I know this to be true."

"How?" Terk set her jaw for an argument.

"Faith."

Using charcoal, Yarwhin drew a drab, dark orb surrounded by clouds and shadows. "Obsid is a place of darkness. Father told us his mother was sent there from Pearlan." He drew a world of white and silver and gold. "Apparently she was set in charge of the world where transgressors went to await redemption. She herself seduced a higher god and conceived Father." He explained that because the higher god already had a mate, that this was a transgression. "The higher god allowed Sabita Ignis, Grandmother, to bear all the blame."

The children leaned closer, listening in rapt attention.

Yarwhin continued. "When word came that the highest gods wanted to send representatives to other worlds, Sabita sought their approval for her son to travel.

"From the gods' observation, Salmyra was a primitive world, yet one that still revered the Elementals. As a matter of fact, it did not even have a name." Yarwhin smiled at the facial expressions on his children.

He drew a world with multiple colors—blue, green, gold, yellow, brown, gray, orange, red— and blended several to give magenta, purple, and various shades in between. Images of trees, flowers, mountains, bodies of water, volcanoes, and ice took shape. Time again stood still, and the likeness resembled pictures from scrolls Illuminet had taught the children to read.

"Father came here and began to walk among the people. He claimed this world as his own. His name was Salmyr Ignis."

5
BROTHERS

TOR wrinkled his brow. "Mamere taught us that our world got its name from one of our ancestors, but she never told us he was a god from some other place."

Yarwhin held up a finger. "Not a god. The son of a god."

"I don't understand," said Terk. "If both his parents were gods, why is he not a god? Two humans make human babies. Two fish make fish babies. I guess even two Danooks make Danook babies."

Lips pursed, Yarwhin drew again. "Gods are a bit different, and the things you call Danooks are a story unto themselves. I'll tell you that also." He drew a male and a female. "Gods, having no known origin, produce winged offspring."

"Your father had wings?" Terk's mouth fell open.

"Yes. I suppose you might refer to them as Angels—or evil ones become Demons. My father was a selfish creature, wanting total control—domination. He, for the purpose of your understanding, was considered a Demon." He gave the young one he drew black wings. He drew another with silvery-white wings and auburn hair. He touched the likeness gently and sighed. "We'll come back to this one."

Yarwhin added the black-winged creature to his depiction of Salmyra. "Father came here. At first, he just lived among the people and accepted their worship and tribute. But then, seeing the beautiful women of the world, he desired more of his kind. The problem, though, came because there were no more of his kind on this world, and he was yet to understand that a hybrid between himself and a human would be something altogether different."

"Do you have wings?" Terk blurted.

"No, I have ridges where wings might have been, but mine never sprouted. My brother's did."

"So," Tor interrupted, "Grandfather took a human for a mate?"

"More than one." Yarwhin nodded. "As many as would yield, and some who did not."

"No!" gasped Tae, her hand flying to her lips.

"Yes." Yarwhin frowned. "Father soon discovered that only very strong human women could carry his child to term. Many died giving birth and all but two of his offspring died. Leviaddan and I have different mothers. It is said that my mother gave herself willingly to Father, and that he loved her. She was a beauty. I've been told I have her appearance. But she died birthing me. Father hated me because he blamed me for her death." A look of utter sadness crossed his handsome face. "Leviaddan's mother was taken against her will, but she lived and was mother to both of us."

"Oh, by the gods!" Terk exclaimed.

Her father bestowed a soft smile on her. "Because she gave him what he so desired, Father set Fayla Norotor up with a lavish life."

Yarwhin started to draw again. Tae touched his hand. "Papere, draw the story on the walls."

"What an excellent suggestion." Yarwhin stood and sketched a castle on a mountain surrounded by clouds. "This is where we lived until the high gods demanded Father's return, but he was forbidden to bring us. Leviaddan and I are considered curses. Father went back to Obsid almost three hundred revolutions of Salmyra. We do not know if he lives or if the gods killed him for his folly. Yet, we learned many of those who ventured beyond created Nephilim on other worlds."

"So, you know how we have felt abandoned?" Terk said with some contrition.

"Indeed, I do. But you three are united. Not so for my brother and me.

"Leviaddan did get wings. He was able to fly to many areas of Salmyra. I, too, journeyed once Fayla died, but I walked or sailed or rode on the backs of a sundry collection of beasts."

"Horsenae?" asked Terk.

"Yes." Yarwhin nodded. "As well as camalia."

"One hump or two?" asked Tae.

"Both."

Enthralled with the drawings and the story, all were startled when the overhang opened of its own accord. A voice bellowed, "So, your little bastards found you! I guess you deserve a bit of company, but now I can search for that bitch who birthed them. My children will gorge on her flesh."

Yarwhin charged the rumbling recess. He pounded the top with his fists. "If you go anywhere near Illuminet, I will kill you!"

The voice laughed and faded away.

***

"That answers your question, Tae," Terk whispered.

Tae jumped to her feet. "He loves Mamere!" She ran to her father's side. "Who was that? Can he hurt Mamere?"

"That!" A slight flicker of gold came into his blue eyes as he pointed. "That was Leviaddan. He can't know where Illuminet is."

"She's…" Terk began.

"Sh!" Yarwhin snapped. "He might be listening."

Tor jumped to his feet. "We have to get back to her."

"I'm trying to figure it out," Yarwhin groaned.

"Why does he want us dead?" Terk demanded.

"He knows you can free me from here."

"Why are you here?" she pried.

Tae took his hand. "Come, Papere. Finish telling us about your brother."

"She's right," said Tor. "The more we know, the better we can fight."

"Your mother has done such a good job with you." Yarwhin sighed and returned to their cushions.

When he was again seated, Terk asked, "Does our *uncle* talk to you often?"

"No. That was only the third time. First, was the day he put me here. The next, was the day he discovered you three had been born. And, now, today. In all these years, I've had one other communication—my grandmother told me where to seek my freedom and counted it her own redemption."

Tor scowled. "You said we are connected." He pointed to his sisters. "But you and your brother weren't. What caused you to be so divided?"

Yarwhin laughed, but there was no mirth. It was a bitter sound. "A woman."

6
THE GREAT DIVIDE

"MAMERE?" asked Tor.

"No. Long before your mother." Yarwhin returned to the outcropping and ordered more food and drink. "We need nourishment."

The children ate as their father talked, the painting forgotten.

"As I told you, Leviaddan had wings. He flew all over Salmyra. He found me on my own travels." He shrugged. "I suppose we had some connection before we disagreed. He found me and began to tell me about his conquests—women and the number of children he'd sired. But then, he grumbled about the weakness of human females and how he thought a different creature could bear stronger children."

Yarwhin abandoned his meal and paced. "Being alone and lonely, I went with my brother. For a while, we stayed together. Every place we went, Leviaddan bedded women, trying to create the perfect child!" He shook his head.

"I asked him how he could be so heartless. How he could have no regard for the well-being of the women and children, most of whom died." He waved a hand. "Oh, he has several offspring that survived, but he, like Father, wanted to dominate Salmyra. He thought producing more and more children was the way. But the cost was just too high."

Yarwhin became quiet and ran a hand over the cold, stone walls.

"Papere," Tae said after a long silence.

"Forgive me." He brushed tears from his cheeks.

"Leviaddan and I traveled to the farthest southern point of Salmyra—Reoite Tundra Theas. The women there were stronger, bigger, healthier. My brother found three women he wanted, and I met Melita Kalt. She was the most beautiful creature I had ever seen. I had vowed not to propagate my father's selfishness. But Melita stole my heart."

He looked each child in the eye. "When you lose your heart, your mind often follows. Yes, I loved Melita."

A ragged breath showed his depth of emotion. "The people of the south had customs Leviaddan ignored. The elders had to approve a coupling. I sought the blessing of Melita's father. It took a great deal of convincing that I was not like my brother. At last, I was successful, and Melita and I wed as was the custom of her people. Some months later, Melita gave me a son, while all three women Leviaddan had impregnated died in childbirth, along with the children.

"Leviaddan became crazed. He swept through the village, slaying any and all. He came to my dwelling and we fought. With his wings, he had an advantage. He took me high in the air and dropped me. The last thing I heard was Melita's wails. When I regained consciousness, only a handful of the village people lived. Leviaddan killed my wife and child. He fled the village. I stayed. These were now my people. But I vowed to never sire children again."

He looked at his three children. Terk cocked her head to the side. "But you have us."

"Yes. And my brother is trying to kill you."

"Why does he hate you?" asked Tor.

"Because the people love me." He buried his face in his hands and wept. "And I let them down. I let my brother almost destroy Salmyra."

***

As of one accord, the three teens wrapped their arms around their father.

"It wasn't your fault, Papere," said Tae.

"Finish your story," Tor encouraged.

Terk ended with, "Then, tell us about Mamere and us."

"I need a break. Please understand." Yarwhin shivered. "I truly need to sleep before I continue."

"Then let's call it a day and pick up after breakfast," Tae said.

Yarwhin lay in his normal spot to sleep. Before he dozed off, he found himself flanked— a daughter on each side and Tor stretched out above his head. They fell asleep, drawing strength from one another.

***

The triplets awoke to a scent they had never smelled. "What is that?" Tor asked leading his sisters to the food their father was setting out.

"Melita called it cinnamon roll-ups. It's yeast bread with butter, sugar, and cinnamon." He pointed at the fruit. "Baked apples."

The teens ate as if they had never tasted food.

Laughing aloud, Yarwhin said, "I'm glad you liked that. I have the energy to tell the rest now. Are you three ready?"

The three used the water closet and settled in to hear the rest of the story.

"You were going to tell us why Leviaddan hates you," spurred Terk with more enthusiasm than she had showed before.

"Yes. My brother was and is jealous that the people accept me and that I found love. All the places I visited before him, I was welcomed, even revered. I never forced myself on the people but acted as one of them. After he left the southernmost people, Leviaddan sought a heartier vessel to bear his children." Yarwhin stood.

"I must digress. You must know that a first-generation Nephilim has the ability to change form."

"Form? As in animals?" asked Tor.

"Yes."

"What can you become?" asked Terk.

"I have only ever changed into a tiggra."

Wide-eyed, Tae asked, "What kind?"

Yarwhin pointed to his hair. "Silver and brown striped."

"So, there might be others?" Tae continued. "Can *we* change?"

"I might have other forms. You—I don't know. But I told you that because of what my brother did."

Yarwhin returned to his seat. "I already told you that once I could wield all the Elemental Powers. So, could Leviaddan. He took them to the extreme—floods, ice storms, raining fire and brimstone, cyclones leveling whole towns. If the humans did not bow to him, he unleashed his wrath. Humans began to fight over which power was the most dangerous. Leviaddan laughed at their gullibility.

"To satisfy his lust, he chose the Wulfgar—thus, your Danooks. They are not survivors of war, but the mixed creatures my brother spawned. They are strong and vicious, but not the most intelligent of creatures. However, they can learn, and do."

Tor nodded. "We saw that. They have figured out how to get past our fencing."

"And the ones you are familiar with are second and third generations." He jutted his chin toward Terk. "As you said, two Danooks make Danook babies. He set them loose on societies that riled him. He also unleashed his Elemental powers, using the power that could devastate most, the most feared for the pain of it—Fire.

"I confess. I hid, stayed with the southerners. I wanted no part of being Nephilim. But I am what I am. Melita's father encouraged me—yea, pushed me to accept my position and to put a stop to Leviaddan's reign of terror.

"I finally overcame my grief and confronted him. Each of us knew that we could only be killed by one of our own kind—that meant each other in this world. I countered every attack he threw, yet he could still fly. The last thing I remember is hearing screams as Leviaddan showered Salmyra with fire so hot it melted those it touched—all life, plant and animal. I saw a blinding flash and woke up here."

He waved his hand back and forth. "The obsidian drains my powers. I'm helpless."

"But you got out of here somehow!" Terk yelled. "You met Mamere. You made us."

"Yes, my darlings. And that is another story."

7
ONCE IN A BLUE MOON

"ANOTHER *story*?" Terk huffed. "I am beginning to think that's all there is—stories."

"Terk!" Tae chastised her sister. "Give Papere a chance to tell us everything."

"And what if it's all lies?" Terk licked her teeth and made a popping sound.

"And what if it's true?" asked Tor, his voice cracking for the first time. He touched his throat.

"You are becoming a man," Yarwhin intoned. Then he turned to Terk. "What can I do to convince you I speak the truth?"

"Tell us something about Mamere—something only her lover would know."

"Something you know as well?" Yarwhin arched an eyebrow. "If only her lover knows, I could lie, and you would never know."

Terk puckered her lips. "Well, of course, we'd have to know."

"Very well." Yarwhin removed the tunic he wore and turned his back to the children. "I've told you I have ridges where my wings never erupted."

"Yes," Tor said. "We see them."

"I also said Illuminet is my Angel. She has something that looks similar, but redder and more ragged, like scars."

"How would we know that?" Terk snapped.

"She does," said Tae quietly. "Mamere never dresses in front of us, but I came upon her after she bathed. I asked what happened to her back, and she told me she'd tell me someday."

"I will tell you," said Yarwhin. "Illuminet is truly my Angel. Her wings were removed."

***

Leaving the children to ponder his revelation, Yarwhin walked to the smaller cavern where the three had landed when they fell. He carried the Fire Brazier to light the way and sat in the center of the room and stared at the ceiling. *How did Leviaddan send us here? It will be seven revolutions before I can leave again, but must they stay? I would never want them trapped here with me. They must go back! It is the only way.*

"Papere?"

The voice startled him. *Not Tae.* He smiled.

"I believe you. Come back and tell us what we need to know."

Terk walked to her father and touched the ridges on his back. "Do they hurt?"

"No. But Leviaddan was in agony while his wings came in."

"I'm sorry."

"There is no reason to be sorry. You're careful. That's a good thing."

"Mamere tells me I need patience with others."

"True, but you're young."

Terk took her father's hand. "Come back. Tell us about you and Mamere. We know you love her. She told us she was chosen and that she's Fire. There's something special about her, but she's never said what. She said she was forbidden. By you?"

"No. The only promise I asked was to let me tell you my story. I thought I'd have to do it once in a blue moon. I was unsure you'd be able to come to me, and I can only leave this place once every ten years and only for one rotation of Salmyra." He squeezed her hand. "Let's go back to the others."

***

Once again settled on the plush black pillows, Yarwhin picked up his explanations. "Somehow my brother trapped me here—I am unsure where *here* is, as Tor asked. I know the obsidian prohibits me from using my powers. On Salmyra I could have blasted a hole through a cave wall with a fireball or used a focused stream of water to wash the wall away. Here, I cannot even produce enough fire to light the torches. They were already lit and never go out."

Tae scowled. "Could this be Obsid?"

Quirking an eyebrow, Yarwhin said, "It is possible."

"So?" Terk pursed her lips in thought. "We could be on a different world altogether?"

Yarwhin shrugged. "Obsid? The place where transgressors go to await judgment? What was my transgression? Loving a human? Sitting by and letting Leviaddan rage? Why is he not imprisoned?" He looked at each child. "I had not considered that my brother might have gone beyond Salmyra."

"Perhaps he lied, Papere," said Tor. "Perhaps many things changed in a millennium."

"True, but we must learn now so we can control the future," Terk declared.

"Yes, and so you shall. I have already told you I have had only a few verbal visits via"— Yarwhin pointed to the outcropping—"that. In the beginning, my meals and clothing were just here each morning. Then, the gurgling sound became clear to me and I was able to speak with whatever entity resides there. You cannot imagine the loneliness and despair." He shook his head. "There were times I wished to die.

"Ten years passed, and the voice bade me come. I looked in and suddenly found myself among Melita's people. Just when I thought I'd been freed, I awoke here again. Time and time again, every decade, I found myself thrown among the people I had come to love and then cast back here.

"Salmyra has a cosmic event every ten years—a blue moon. On that day alone, I am allowed out of here."

"We saw that!" Tor exclaimed. "On our tenth birthday. Just after we arrived at…" He snagged a piece of charcoal and canvas and wrote L-I-B-R-E-T-A-N-T-E. "Just in case Uncle Levi is listening."

Yarwhin laughed—a full, deep belly laugh.

The girls giggled. After a full minute, Tae said, "The Danooks went wild that night. Mamere double barred the doors and extinguished all the tallows."

Terk nodded. "And to help us fall asleep, she told us about a beautiful man that would one day restore Salmyra, and we wouldn't have to be afraid." She looked her father in the eye. "You."

Tor went on, "But the sky was so pretty. The moon was full and looked like a giant sapphire. The whole sky glowed a pastel azure."

"I dreamed I saw the beautiful man that night," said Tae. "But I couldn't move to touch him."

"Mamere sang," Terk murmured. "That hypnotic song. We weren't supposed to wake." She shot her father a look.

"Yes," he said. "I saw you that night. You were all so perfect. Taekeyla opened her eyes." He smiled. "You didn't dream me, dear one.

"Humans on Salmyra carry children within for a full year. You were created beneath a blue moon, and I saw you—my blessings—under a blue moon. It was actually your ninth physical birthday, but Salmyrans count the year within the womb."

Yarwhin lifted a cushion and held it against his chest, closing his eyes. "I held Illuminet in my arms. The blue moon became what I lived for."

He took a deep breath and laid the pillow down. "Five times I was thrust into the southernmost kingdom, just to be sent back here. Then, the one other voice came to me. She told me my next day of freedom I would be sent to Lumensca and there I would find my miracle to gain my freedom. All I had to do was lean into my provider's mist.

"Lumenesca." His voice broke and he stared at the painting of the castle in the clouds. "The majestic place where I grew up—pearly white castle almost floating in the clouds…"

Yarwhin buried his face in the cushion.

Tor touched his father's shoulder. "It's real?" he asked. "Not myth?"

"Yes. It was the most spectacular place."

"Was?" Tor mumbled.

"When I got there, the castle was near rubble, silver and golden lights extinguished, a city of thousands reduced to perhaps a hundred. The pristine snow looked like ash.

"I heard the cry of an infant and followed the sound. A wizened old woman rocked a rickety cradle in which lay the most angelic baby, light radiating from her. The old woman crooked her finger toward me, and I followed her beckoning.

The old woman said, 'Behold Illuminet, your salvation.'"

"What?" barked Terk. "Mamere?"

"Yes." Yarwhin nodded. "I know I looked at the old lady as if she must have been a lunatic. 'A baby?' I shouted.

"'An Angel,' the woman said. 'My charge. In time you will grow to love her, and she will give you what you need to escape your prison.'

"I sat and stared at the child the entire rotation of Salmyra. She gurgled and cooed and smiled.

"Then, I was back here. Ten years later, I was thrown back to Lumenesca. Illuminet had grown into an active, vibrant girl. She showed me the fireballs she could create in her palms.

"The old mother talked to me again and told me Illuminet only possessed one Elemental, and it was not strong. Yet, she would retrieve the Fire Brazier of Lavan—one of four items I must have to break out of here." He pointed to the Fire Brazier he carried when he left the main chamber.

"Ten more years passed. Illuminet showed me the majestic wings she'd sprouted." He touched the auburn-haired Angel he'd painted earlier. "Her guardian spoke with me again, saying that the mate of the god Sabita, my grandmother, had seduced, felt deep remorse since the basic banishment of my grandmother and her child had ultimately resulted in the decimation of Salmyra. In her guilt, she herself had chosen a lesser god and had a child— Illuminet. She sent the child to Salmyra to help reclaim and restore the world.

"'How?' I asked.

"'You must defeat your brother, but you can never do it alone. You must possess the four Elemental Relics to restore your power. Illuminet can get only one for you, but she can give you the means to procure the other three.'

"I was repulsed!" Yarwhin clenched his fists and ground his teeth. "Illuminet, so beautiful, so kind, so innocent, was no more than a pawn to assuage a goddess's guilt. I left that blue moon, anger boiling in my chest.

"Again, I was sent to Lumenesca. Illuminet herself talked to me. She accepted her destiny. Her hand to my cheek sent a pulse throughout my body.

"Suddenly, Illuminet's guardian rushed in. 'He's here to kill our Angel. We must flee. Next blue moon, ask the mist to send you to Illuminet.'

"They vanished through a secret passage that lead deep inside the mountain.

"Leviaddan charged in and sent me flying. I was still so weak. Blow after blow, Leviaddan demanded to know Illuminet's whereabouts. I truly did not know, but I would have died before I revealed anything to him.

"Then, I was back here, bruised and beaten. The provider gave me healing herbs and ointment.

"Another blue moon sent me to a village covered in snow. There was no longer a guardian. Illuminet was alone, the only mother she'd ever known, dead.

"Thrice more, the blue moon came before my heart exploded with love for Illuminet. We gave in to the passion we both felt.

"After that, ten years felt like eons, just to touch her, to hold her.

"The second decade after that, what I found rent my heart in two. Illuminet handed me the Fire Brazier of Lavan, but what the Lavanians did to her!" A sob caught in Yarwhin's throat.

"Her sacrifice only made me love her more. Blue moon after blue moon, our love grew stronger. We sought the elders of the village to sanctify our union, and when we did…"

Yarwhin sprang to his feet. "When we had a blessed coupling, there came the three of you, although I did not even know about you until I found my love the next blue moon.

"But if Leviaddan found out we had mated, I feared the worst; so, I told Illuminet to find"— He put a finger to his lips—"the secret place and to wait for me there. Thus, she fled and traveled until she was there, and that is where I saw you for the first time."

He let out a long, weighty sigh. "And, yes, my children, I love your mother with all my being."

8
FIRE BRAZIER OF LAVAN

THE triplets bombarded Yarwhin with questions... "How did someone hurt Mamere...How did she get the Fire Brazier of Lavan...Why can't Mamere use her powers...What do you need to be free?"

Yarwhin held up his hand. "Patience." He lifted the Fire Brazier of Lavan.

With a deep sigh, he said, "When Illuminet first manifested her use of fire, the gods had already limited her abilities. Full strength was always contingent upon her helping to restore me." He closed his eyes. "She thought that once she obtained the Fire Brazier she would be endowed fully. Illuminet's true strength, as with Angels of all kind, lies within her wings."

In a wave effect, each triplet popped a hand over their mouths to keep from exclaiming.

Yarwhin gave a slow, deliberate nod. "Her abilities are even weaker. She can barely start a cook fire." He fisted his hands. "I get so angry every time I think about it." He plunked down the Fire Brazier.

He clasped his hands behind his back and paced. After a long moment he brought a fist to his mouth and dropped his hands to his sides. "I wish I could mind-mergence with you, but inside these"—He placed a hand on the shiny black surface nearest him—"walls, I cannot. It would be so much easier to show you than tell you, and I cannot begin to share Illuminet's real pain."

"Papere," Tor said, "sit down and tell us what you can. Knowing what happened to Mamere could help us when our time comes."

Yarwhin made eye contact with his son. "You look so much like your mother. I cringe inside when I think about any of you putting yourselves in danger. Yet, I know it's the only way to freedom and to save Salmyra. Forgive me my folly."

"It's not all on you, Papere," Terk said. "I suppose we could refuse to go in search of anything."

A low chuckle preceded, "I suppose you could." Yarwhin sat back down. "Yes, Terkoyze, you are headstrong. It might keep you alive."

Terk lowered her eyes and blushed.

"Very well," Yarwhin said. "Illuminet found the wicket to Lavan."

"Wicket?" Tae interrupted.

"Ah, yes." Yarwhin scratched his scalp. "I forgot that part. All the worlds are connected by wickets—a means to travel great distances in short time." He turned toward the overhang. "Perhaps you are correct, and this is Obsid. If that thing is a wicket, it's controlled elsewhere. And I know not by whom."

"You think Leviaddan has something to do with it, Papere?" asked Terk.

"Most likely."

"Then we won't be going anywhere soon." Tae pursed her lips. "Tell us about Mamere and Lavan and what's required of us."

A smile spread across Yarwhin's face. "My Angel has done so well with the three of you. There is no malice in her." He reclined on some of the multitude of cushions.

"Illuminet discovered the wicket to Lavan after crossing a few others. Lavan is a desolate world. Very little plant life thrives there, for most of the place is active volcanoes. The few towns are far apart and their inhabitants warlike and barbaric. The place is shrouded in a cloud of ash, thicker than anything you've seen on Salmyra. Yet, their sun boils the atmosphere, and the people drink hot water."

"Are they human?" asked Tor.

"Humanoid." Yarwhin arched an eyebrow. "They are often described as descendants of Demons. They are said to be of deep bronze skin, dark fathomless eyes, and straight black hair."

"All of them?" Tae mimicked her father's raised eyebrow to perfection.

"So, I am told." Yarwhin nodded. "I have never seen them. Legend holds that the males tend to be tall and wiry and some are winged, but their wings are small, not strong enough to carry them far. The women are said to be smaller and very few have wings.

"So, of course, when Illuminet crossed the threshold, she, with her porcelain skin, and fiery red hair, not to mention her downy wingspan, stood out in sharp contrast."

Yarwhin spread his arms wide as if to show Illuminet's wingspan.

"She was immediately brought before the elders of the nearest village. Illuminet told them who she was and explained her quest.

"The rulers laughed at her, but they told her if she could descend into the heart of Conflatile Montem, which means Molten Mountain, without being burned alive, she could have the Fire Brazier of Lavan. The religious leaders, notably the Shaman of the town, went on to tell her they believed if the Fire Brazier could be removed from the heart of the volcano, their world would become more docile and productive. They believed the gods had cursed them with its presence.

"Seeing an opportunity to assist with more than one cause, Illuminet was happy to help."

"Of course, she was. That's Mamere," Tae said.

Her siblings nodded agreement, and Yarwhin continued.

"As they spoke, the ground trembled, and lava rolled down the sides of Conflatile Montem. The leaders told Illuminet she had one full rotation of their world to get to the Fire Braizer before another eruption.

"Your mother sprang into action, running outside and unfurling her wings. The brilliance that radiated from her and the coolness offered in the shade of her wings sent the people into screams of terror. They had never seen anything so lovely or so frightening.

"The rulers laid hands on her, demanding her wings."

"No!" Terk cried, tears smarting her eyes.

"Illuminet told them they could take her most breathtaking feature once she retrieved the Fire Brazier. They let her go, and she flew into the heat and flames and bubbling, molten lava. Down, down, down she glided through a narrow passage, her wings getting singed often and her lungs burning from the stench of brimstone.

"At last, she spotted the Fire Brazier in a cylindrical alcove behind a flowing fall of lava. She landed and carefully picked her way toward the cascade, though the ground seared her feet. She wrapped her wings around her and plunged through the flowing lava."

None of the children dared breathe as their father related their mother's exploits.

"Once behind the curtain of magma, the temperature moderated and the air became breathable. She lifted the Fire Brazier, and the volcano quaked.

"Illuminet shot out the passage with all the speed she could muster. High into the air she soared, balls of fire following her.

"Then, all became quiet. Conflatile Montem changed from glowing melted orange to obsidian, darker and harder than these walls in an instant."

Yarwhin breathed hard, struggling with the painful memory Illuminet had shared with him.

"Your mother returned to the village and the Shaman reached for the Fire Brazier. She withheld it from his grasp, telling him to take what he had demanded.

"Screaming obscenities and profanities, the elders again grabbed her. They tied her down and the Shaman used an obsidian blade to slice her wings from her back. He left her to die, to bleed to death, and took the Fire Brazier, too."

Yarwhin heard the quiet sobs and sniffles of his children. He fought back his own tears.

"Some time later, when all was dark, a lone female crept to Illuminet with a red-hot rod. She cauterized the gaping wounds. Illuminet begged her to get the Fire Brazier. The woman beckoned her to follow with only hand motions.

"Weak from blood loss, Illuminet crawled after the woman. At a stone structure, the woman pointed. Illuminet crept through the doorway. On a mat, the Shaman snored. The Fire Brazier rested on a pedestal. Fire from it flowed into the veins of the vile man.

"Illuminet managed to produce a fireball and placed it on the spot where the fire entered the Shaman. She lifted the Fire Brazier and backed out the door."

The children sat erect and wide-eyed.

"Seeing the fear in her rescuer's eyes, Illuminet took the small woman's hand and led her to the wicket. By the time they reached the way home, the village had come to life and knew Illuminet, the Fire Brazier, and Dawn, as your mother called the woman, were gone.

"As angry voices approached, Illuminet and Dawn stepped through the wicket.

"On the other side, Illuminet drew from her last fiber of power and set a constant fire at the wicket. Either the Lavanians did not know how to use it or were too afraid. Either way, Illuminet had this thing." He touched the Fire Brazier. "Dawn slipped away in the night once Illuminet gave it to me."

Tears streamed down the faces of the triplets. Tor struggled to speak. "Do you think Leviaddan got to the Shaman?"

"I don't know, but he will do whatever he thinks necessary to keep me from having any hope. I think it's possible the people on Lavan are Drows, not Demons."

"Whats?" Tor said.

"Evil Elves. And if, indeed, they are winged, perhaps part fairy. I never heard of an Elf with wings."

Tae laid her hand on Yarwhin's arm. "But you do have hope, Papere. We're here."

"Dear one, I cannot promise your sacrifice not to be greater,"

"It matters not." Terk stood. "This is our destiny."

9
HOPE

"YOUR destiny." Yarwhin buried his face in his hands. "How I wish it did not have to be." He raised his head and gazed at his children with teary eyes. "But you are Salmyra's only hope."

"Papere," Tor said, his voice cracking again. His sisters giggled, happy that their puberty did not have such embarrassing indications.

Yarwhin gave them a rueful smirk. He sensed they might tease their brother, but if anyone else did, Tor's tormentors would face dire consequences.

"Girls," Yarwhin chided.

"Sorry," Terk said behind her hand, "but one second he sounds like a squeaky bird, then the next like you, and back to sounding like us."

Tae patted her brother's shoulder. "Sorry."

Tor shrugged. "I might recall where to find that million-legged creature you fear when we get out of here."

"Tor!" Tae shrieked.

Yarwhin's smile disappeared. "Yes. Getting you out of here…"

"Worry about that tomorrow. Now tell us what we must do for our world," said Terk, suddenly serious.

"As you wish." Their father gave a nod. "I think you are all aware of the Elemental power you'll be able to wield. But for me to escape this place, I must have three more sacred items in my possession. All are hidden on different worlds. I know not which ones. That's what Illuminet has tried to discover."

"So," Tor said, knitting his brow. "You don't know where we must go, but you do know what we must find."

"Yes."

"So, tell us, and we can help Mamere study," Tae encouraged.

Terk suggested, "Perhaps putting our minds together here might yield clues."

"Perhaps," Yarwhin concurred. "Indeed."

Yarwhin took up paints again. He hastily drew the Fire Brazier of Lavan. "The four relics are associated with each Elemental. Illuminet has found and delivered the first."

He drew a plume in exaggerated proportion. "The wind Elemental is a feather from The Great White Eagle, Iolar Mór Bán, freely given."

"A bird's feather?" Tor asked with arched eyebrow.

"Not just any bird," Yarwhin corrected. "And not just any feather. No one knows where Iolar Mór Bán resides these days. Iolar Mór Bán is the size of a dragon and more ill-tempered. You would be a mere snack to him."

Yarwhin held up a finger. "To draw Iolar Mór Bán to scale, I would need a mountain. I do know his plumes must be kept moist, but not rained upon. Thus, logic would dictate a nest in high mountain peaks, surrounded by clouds, but where rain never falls."

"Nowhere on Salmyra," Tor observed.

"No," Yarwhin affirmed. "And, Tor, you cannot get a molted feather or pluck a feather—The latter would make you dinner for certain. You must convince Iolar Mór Bán to give you a plume."

Laughing softly, Tae said, "Are you sure this Iolar Mór Bán is male?"

"Not exactly," Yarwhin admitted. "Why?"

She grinned toward her brother. "Tornabolt sort of has a charm with the girls we've been around."

"Then, if Iolar Mór Bán is a nesting female, that could work to his advantage." Yarwhin gave his son a wink and Tor felt the burning blush to the roots his dark hair.

Terk released a long breath. "I'm glad that's not my quest. I'd be too impatient."

"Yes, my darling, you would," her father agreed. "But your artifact is a treasure indeed."

"A treasure?" Terk's mouth dropped open.

"Yes." Yarwhin nodded and drew again, depicting a multi-colored chalice. "You must find the Goblet of Godetta, said to have held the tears of Godetta herself as she gave her life for her children."

"We read her story," Terk said. "She was not human, but reptilian. Her scales were of numerous gems. Rather than allow her children to be slaughtered, she melted, and her blood covered them so that their assassins could no longer see them. Her scales covered the universe in jewels."

"Yes, you learned your lessons well. It is believed Godetta was not just any reptile, but a dragon. It is believed that tears shed into the cup take on healing powers. The Goblet of Godetta is encrusted with her jeweled scales. Many a looter would kill to possess it."

"Treasure is often buried to be protected," Terk mused.

"It's buried somewhere," Tae suggested. "Deep."

Yarwhin agreed. "That stands to reason."

"Great," Terk muttered. "Some deep, dark cave filled with Danooks."

Yarwhin could not stifle his chuckle. "Soon, Danooks will flee before you. You need not fear your cousins."

"Well, maybe there aren't any on the world where the Goblet is hidden," Tor said.

"That could well be." Yarwhin gave his son a smile.

"My Elemental is water," Tae blurted. "What must I find?"

"The proverbial needle in a haystack," Yarwhin replied with a heavy sigh.

"What?"

"Godetta's tears themselves," Yarwhin murmured.

"The best place to hide water is in water," Tor said, his voice shallow for the scope of the search.

Tae's face scrunched in worry. "A water world? Or worse! Tears could be scattered on multiple worlds. My task seems impossible!"

"That is my concern, dear one," Yarwhin intoned.

10
WICKET

"NOTHING is impossible if we put our minds together!" declared Terk.

"Your optimism and determination are treasures themselves," Yarwhin said.

Tor wiggled his eyebrows. "Yes, both my sisters are rare gems."

"Oh, yes, big brother," Terk teased, "and I'm sure you're an unrefined lump of coal."

"Still," Tae said, her voice sober. "We can't do anything here."

"True," Yarwhin said with a yawn.

Her voice filled with concern, Tae said, "You're tired." Then, she yawned.

Yarwhin's eyes drooped, and he fell over, asleep. Tae joined him.

Terk sprang to her feet. "Help me, Tor! Leviaddan's doing something to this chamber. Help me get them out of here."

Tor swayed when he stood but grabbed one of his father's arms. "Papere first. He's too heavy for either of us."

Together, Terk and Tor wrangled Yarwhin to the second chamber. They sat for a moment where the air was cooler, taking deep, cleansing breaths.

Tor mumbled, "Now that we're here, I realize there was a cloying odor in the other room."

"Me too."

Yarwhin groaned.

Tor pulled his tunic over his mouth and nose. "Cover up. Let's get Tae."

Their sister was much easier to move. Tae rested beside her father and the other two leaned against the cool stone wall. "I'm tired too," Terk confessed.

"Perhaps it's late," Tor said. "A nap can do no harm."

***

Many moments later, all awoke to a female voice. "Yarwhin. Yarwhin. You can return to the main chamber. I've cleared the poppy oil from the air."

"Grandmother?"

"Yes. Leviaddan will never learn. I am a goddess. He cannot hide your or his actions from me. Now, return to the overhang and bring my great-grandchildren. We must talk. Leviaddan will try to circumvent my interference. I cannot free you, but he did not send the children to you—I did."

"We're coming."

They all stirred and stretched. "Come, children," Yarwhin commanded in a gentle voice.

The triplets followed their father. All approached the outcropping.

"Hello, little ones," the woman's voice said. "I am Sabita Ignis. I brought you to your father. Now he has told you what is required of you. You can escape here, and you can return here. Hopefully, you will have completed your quests before Salmyra's next blue moon."

None of the triples spoke for a long moment. Then, Terk said, "How do we get out of here?"

"Patience," Tor muttered. "This is our great-grandmother."

Sabita laughed and her voice wafted across a great expanse. "I understand the desire to begin. Listen to me. You must learn all you can before you start. Stay one more day with Yarwhin, and I shall send you where you can continue your education."

"How do we leave?" asked Tae.

"Here, sweet one. You just need to step in at exactly the same moment—as with all wickets. If you go one at a time, you could end up in different places. Tomorrow at this time, I will have your destination wicket open." Her voice faded away.

11
AWAKE IN BED

THE triplets, as well as their father, slept very little that evening. The next morning, Yarwhin made sure a hot breakfast met them.

Tae stirred the thick ginger porridge. "I'm not hungry."

"You must eat, dear one," Yarwhin coaxed.

Terk said what her sister thought. "What if we never see you again?"

"I'm certain we shall be together in the end."

"What if Sabita lied?" Tor asked. "What if entering that thing"—He pointed to the overhang—"takes us directly to our uncle?"

"It won't." The voice came from the swirling mist.

"Gran Sabita," Terk, the most outspoken, said, "exactly where is *here*? We might need to know if we're ever to return."

"Oh, my lovelies," Sabita cooed. "Terk, you are much like me, strong-willed. Be careful not to be too stubborn and weigh your words before you utter them. It is often preferable to walk away from a fight.

"Tae, trust should be earned. Take caution with new acquaintances. Guard your heart.

"And Tor." She sighed. "You have the quiet strength of Yarwhin but also his tendency to feel responsible for all those around you. You cannot save them all—yet. You might have to make hard choices. Draw from your sisters."

"You didn't answer my question," Terk said.

"Here? Here is the place that grants your greatest desire or preys on your greatest fear."

"Riddles!" huffed Terk.

"This place is known as Sárú Saoil Cuardaigh Anan." Sabita never became angry. "Where it is, I do not know, someplace between Pearlan and Obsid, between Heaven and Hell. Somewhere, nowhere, everywhere. Even the angriest of gods hesitate to send anyone here. And only the person who sends you here can free you without the power of all the Elementals. Dearest, it is an enigma even to me. But to banish your own flesh and blood to this place tells me that Leviaddan is truly demented. I am so sorry. I had no clue my folly would lead to such chaos and turmoil."

Tae whispered, "Leviaddan made his own decisions."

"And so, he did," Sabita said. "And now you must decide to step into the mist or not."

The triplets retrieved their packs. "Gran Sabita," Tor said, "we need supplies."

"No, you don't. Trust me," she replied.

In turn, the three hugged their father. Tae held on to him the longest. "We *will* be back."

Yarwhin kissed her on top of the head. "I know you will. And if not before the next blue moon, I'll come to you."

They stood before the outcropping and watched the mist swirl. Sabita's voice said, "Remember, all at one time."

In unison, the teens placed one foot into the fog. Their feet felt boggy, like when they had been sucked into the abyss.

Yarwhin reached out a hand toward his children. They began to waver as a mirage.

"I love you, Papere," Terk called. The others seemed to echo her sentiment.

And they vanished into the cloud.

***

No weight. Simply floating. The triplets settled into hypnotic sleep. How long they were in suspended animation, they did not know. There was no fear—only peace. No anxiety—only calm. They seemed to nestle onto a down bed.

The scream from Illuminet shot the triplets straight up from a sound sleep. "Where did you come from?" their mother shrieked.

12
A GENTLE BREEZE

TOR stammered, "W-w-we're in our own beds." He scratched his head and rubbed his eyes.

"Mamere," Tae said, "how long were we gone?"

"Did we ever *leave*?" Terk interjected.

Illuminet finally caught her breath and sank into a woven chair. "Months," she puffed out. "You turned fourteen."

Tor shook his head in disbelief. "It was only a couple of weeks, a month at the most."

"Maybe time is different there," Tae surmised, dipping one eyebrow.

"Where did you…How?" Illuminet waved her hand, palm up. "I only went to the second level a few minutes ago." She sat forward. "How's Yarwhin? You did see him, didn't you?"

"Calm, Mamere." Tor stood and hugged his mother. His sisters followed his example.

"Yes, we saw Papere," Tae said with a big smile.

Illuminet's eyes lit up. "He is extraordinary."

"He loves you too," Terk chimed in.

Her mother turned toward her. "Where is he?"

Tor puffed out a long breath. "Sabita called it Sárú Saoil Cuardaigh Anan."

"Sabita?" Illuminet shrilled, half rising in fear. "She's there?"

"Not physically," Tae said. "She speaks through the mist."

Iluminet scowled. "Mist?"

"We have much to tell." Tor put his arm around his mother's shoulders. She noted he had grown taller.

***

Illuminet listened intently to all her children told her. She was appalled to discover why Danooks existed but overjoyed to find out Sabita was aiding Yarwhin as much as she could. She nodded. "A place of soul-searching? At least Yarwhin has a soul."

Sitting on the floor around a low table, the family dined on dried fruit and roasted doose. After a bite, Terk observed, "Papere eats well, yet he's miserable."

Licking his lips, Tor said, "I'd give up good food for freedom. That's what Papere wants, too."

"Yes." Tae nodded vigorously. "When we succeed in freeing him, he will put the world to rights."

Their mother sighed. "Then I suppose we should begin serious study. You must learn control."

Tor drummed his fingers on the table. "Mamere, I've been thinking."

"What, my son?"

"We all need to learn control, that's true. But it might be easier to focus on one at a time."

"And I suppose you want to go first!" Terk snapped.

"Yes." He looked his sister in the eye. "I think Papere showed us the order we must train. Me first, then you, and Tae last. Our two tasks are daunting, but hers…"

"Nearly impossible," Tae finished. She looked up from studying her fingers. "Tor's right. I will need the two of you to help me. It could be that you have to use your powers to help me isolate Godetta's tears."

Illuminet affirmed, "You will have to work together for each quest, but, I dare say, Tae's looks overwhelming. Even if Terk somehow managed to remove salt, tears are still liquid."

"If," Tae went on with her mother's train of thought, "they are, indeed, in the ocean."

Terk chewed her bottom lip. "I say let's get to work, train, and learn. We can all work on our power and control, but, Mamere, work closest with Tor for now. Let's get ready to soar on the wings of an eagle!"

***

By day's end, Illuminet had pulled every scroll on wind and weather. As the teens stared at the stacks, slack-jawed, she puckered her lips and frowned.

"If we begin intensive training," she said, "Leviaddan might detect our whereabouts."

"Would he come or send Danooks?" Tae asked.

Illuminet's laugh trilled. "Leviaddan is a coward. He will *always* send his minions after you."

Terk asked, "What about you?"

Patting her daughter's cheek, Illuminet said, "What did your father tell you about Nephilim?"

Tor said, "They can only be killed by one of their own kind."

"Exactly." Illuminet nodded. "The same is true for Angels. The Danooks cannot harm me, but they can you because you're both offspring of Nephilim."

"What about our *uncle*?" Terk sneered.

"He could harm you, but he knows now that he cannot kill *me*. As far as I know, I'm the only one of my kind on Salmyra—if your grandfather has not returned. I do fear that he would side with Leviaddan if he did."

"And he has wings," Tor thought aloud.

Absentmindedly, Illuminet touched her back where her wings should have been. She swiped away an unwanted tear.

The teens looked from one to the other, realizing they had seen their mother do this often, but had not known why.

Trying not to draw attention to the strain that Illuminet's missing wings caused, "Can we not fortify this place?" Terk asked.

Illuminet arched her eyebrow. "What do you have in mind?"

"Something Yggamay suggested." Terk marched out the door, followed by her family.

She circled the library four times, which took a full two hours. Her first circle began a hundred yards from the entrance. As she walked, she spread her hands. With each pass, thick vines with briars sprang up. She stopped and spoke to her siblings. "I need seven circles—the number of completion. These need to be made fireproof—Tae."

Tae's brow formed a deep V. "Okay." Ducking and twisting, she made her way among the thorns and whispered. A coating of moisture formed.

Illuminet shot a small fireball at one section. The flame sizzled, and then fizzled.

Terk stared at her brother. "A little help, please, or this will take all day."

Tor laughed and blew toward his sister. The last three circles finished with the speed of the wind.

Finally, standing only a few feet from the entrance, Terk began twisting. Tor breathed on her to pick up speed. Tae covered her in a fine mist. Terk disappeared into the ground. Moments later, she called to her mother and siblings, who peered into the hole she had made. "I'm inside."

She held her hands as if beckoning. "Our protection and our way in and out."

When the rest of the family reached her, Terk put a hand on her brother's shoulder. "Now get busy."

***

They sat around the rough-hewn table with a dozen scrolls unrolled. Illuminet said, "I saw what you can do working together. Now, Tor, let's see what you can do alone, in case you get separated." She turned to her daughters. "Girls, find something to do."

Grumbling, but obeying, the girls left their brother to work.

Tor and Illuminet read through writing after writing over a period of several weeks. Finally, she suspended a cradle from a bar set into two triangles with indentions at the apex for a rod. "Rock the cradle," she said.

Tor gusted a breath. Scrolls flew across the room. The cradle toppled over. He blew out a second frustrated breath, which pinned Illuminet against the wall.

"Mamere!" he shouted, and when he stopped blowing, she slid to the floor.

She smoothed the wrinkles in her clothes and tucked loose strands of auburn hair into the leather thong that held her tresses in place. "Iolar Mór Bán will not be won by might, but by persuasion and gentleness." Illuminet righted the cradle.

She looked sternly at Tor. "Blow the scrolls back in place. Concentrate on the desired outcome."

Barely cracking his lips, Tor targeted each scroll separately until all were back on the table and opened to where they had been reading.

"Good," his mother said. "Now, rock the cradle."

Again, he blew out a breath. Nothing moved. His sisters burst through the door. "By the gods, Tor!" Terk bellowed. "Are you trying to blow us into the mouths of the Danooks that are swarming?"

Tor cast his eyes toward the rush-covered floor. "Sorry."

Illuminet patted her son's hand. "We've worked for weeks. It's almost dark. We'll practice more tomorrow." She got up and lit two tallows.

Tae said, "We brought in taro roots, and we found nesting clucks with eggs."

"That will make a good supper." Illuminet smiled.

"I put a hedge around the clucks," Terk boasted. "I didn't want the Danooks to eat them."

"Good thinking," their mother replied. She set about making their evening meal.

***

Sometime during the night, a soft squeaking awoke Illuminet. She lit a single tallow and followed the sound.

Tor sat on the floor in front of the cradle, which swayed back and forth.

"What are you doing?" she asked.

"Rocking the cradle." He turned to face his mother, and the cradle stopped moving. He gave her a radiant smile. "I had to be calm myself," he explained.

"You've done well." She looked out a window and saw golden streaks on the horizon. "Morning approaches." She gathered cracked barley and dried berries to make breakfast.

When the sun crested the horizon, Tae and Terk ambled in. They all sat down to eat. Terk mopped sweat from her brow. "This is going to be a miserably hot day," she grumbled.

"Let's see about that," Tor said, and he closed his eyes. A gentle breeze began to stir, and light rain fell.

The family stepped outside, still protected by the thorn circles, the rain barely dripping on them. Tor blew gently on the thick vines. The tiny green leaves fluttered. The air cooled.

Illuminet clapped and brought her clasped hands to her lips. "I think you have the gentle breeze. Now you need to know *when* to use a mighty wind."

13
A MIGHTY WIND

THE family strolled back inside, feeling relief. Illuminet said to all three children, "Beyond your Elemental powers, you must also learn two other necessary abilities—all of you."

"What are they, Mamere?" Tae asked.

"One—diplomacy. You must learn to state your needs and wants without getting angry." She made a pointed stare at Terk.

Terk defended herself. "I've gotten better."

"She has," Tor affirmed. "Papere even said so."

"What's the other, Mamere?" Tae asked.

"Compassion. Often, leniency trumps harshness and can profit you loyalty."

"How do you tell the proper time to show mercy?" Tor asked.

Illuminet placed a hand on her son's shoulder. "Follow your heart."

"And if I'm wrong?"

She smiled softly. "We all make mistakes, just like I did on Lavan."

***

Having mastered a gentle breeze and refreshing rain, Tor worked diligently to find the point where it would be necessary to wreak havoc—a cyclone, a hailstorm, a tsunami. Day after day, he ventured farther from the safety of the library so that he could practice calling on his Elemental power for destruction, making sure no one was nearby to be injured in the wake of severe weather. He found he could surround himself with a protective shield. He learned quickly after hailstones left him bruised and with a doose egg on his head. Tae and Terk had laughed, and Illuminet had rebuked them, reminding them that their intensive training was coming.

Early one morning, Tor got up long before his sisters. Illuminet stirred the cracked barley, adding sprigs of mint. "Good morning," she greeted her son.

"Mamere." He kissed her cheek.

She stood straight and cupped her hand around his neck. "You have gotten so tall."

"Papere is gigantic."

"True. You probably won't get that tall."

He began to pack a sack.

"What are you doing?" Illuminet asked.

He paused. "There have been few travelers lately, but the Danooks have increased."

"Leviaddan might have found us."

"Perhaps. Mamere, I'm going beyond the salt dome."

"You'll have to make camp!" She stopped mashing berries to add to the barley.

Tor nodded. "Yes. And I'm going alone."

"Tor!"

"It's time." He looked over his shoulder. "And I'm going before they wake up. Don't let them follow me."

He snagged a cluster of scuppernongs and a slice of bread. "I'm going. Don't worry." He slipped out the door before she could protest.

***

Tor traveled all day until he reached the gypsum-colored embankment where his mother came periodically to harvest salt crystals. From the crest where they watched travelers, the place was more than half a day's walk.

Taking a determined breath, he pulled two spikes from his pack and began to climb the mound. The sun was getting low, but he thought a camp atop the dome would be safest.

Just as he rounded the summit, screams and howls made him freeze. Below, he beheld something he never thought he would see.

Moments before Danooks would come from their burrows, humans entered the creatures' holes with spears, swords, hatchets. Danooks ran into the sunlight, covered their faces with hairy hands, and yowled as blisters instantly burst onto fleshy parts of their bodies, not covered with hair. As the creatures cowed before their greatest enemy, humans rent them asunder.

This is wrong!

An infant Danook ran from a burrow, not on all-fours, but upright. Tor squinted toward the youngster. Close behind the child, a flaxen-haired female followed—shouting at the child, "Run! Keep running! Don't stop!"

Clear, understandable words. She looks more human than canine.

A marauding human charged toward the little one, who froze in terror.

"No!" Tor shouted, seeing the young woman fall over the child.

Tor lifted his hands skyward as the deep crimson blood of Danooks soaked into the sand. Lightning flashed. Thunder boomed. Torrential rain fell. Hailstones pounded both humans and Danooks. Around the woman and child, wind swirled, sending their pursuers sailing, but never touching them.

The intensity of the wind increased. Tor descended the mound, a fluctuating silvery aura repelling the inclement weather.

Fleeing humans and Danooks paused in search of shelter to watch Tor pass through the storm, unharmed. He entered the protective vortex around the young woman and child and stared at the female.

She's no older than me.

In a ball over the child, the young woman cried, "Please! Please spare us."

"I won't hurt you."

The woman raised her head. Two blue orbs brimming tears gazed in amazement at Tor and took in what was happening around her. "Who are you?"

"Tor Ignis." He held out his hand. "If you want to survive, come with me."

He took in the young woman's appearance and the little one she sheltered. *Only small protrusion of nose and upper lip. The child even less prominent. Only a thin mane of fur on her neck and upper arms. The baby, none. Hands with thumbs—no paws. The little one has normal, human feet. The girl—She's beautiful—only a tiny pad on her heel. She's built like Tae and Terk.* He suddenly averted his eyes. *Still naked though—but she looks human.*

"Who are *you*?" he asked.

"Danooks do not have names."

"Danooks do not speak."

She looked down at the little one. "My father called me Fuascailt. He said I was his redemption. But I have not seen him in three revolutions—the night he gave me"—She caressed the little boy's head—"Iontus."

Tor ground his teeth. "Your *father* mated with you?"

"He said he had to correct his mistake."

"Leviaddan?"

She nodded. "He has not followed us when we migrated. I think I did not satisfy him."

"How could you not? He should never have come to you. That is so *wrong!*" He clenched and unclenched his fists. "Your mother—you—and he's probably traipsing across Salmyra and doing the same thing to other packs. He probably plans to try and start a new species." He looked down. "Thank the gods you have a son, but Leviaddan would likely want to breed him with a cousin."

"He would take my child?" She held the little boy close to her breast.

"Not if I have anything to say about it."

Tor held his hand out again. "Come with me. I'll keep you and your son safe."

"How?"

He gave her a smile. "I am Tornabolt Ignis— Wielder of Wind and Weather Elemental." He moved his other hand back and forth, palm up. "Look around you."

"But if we leave the shelter of this— whatever this is—the others will tear you to shreds. Darkness has fallen."

"Can you travel by day?"

She nodded.

Tor bit his lip. "Do you—um—have clothes?"

"What are clothes?"

He lifted his sleeve. "Covering for your body."

She finally saw her nakedness. Color rose high on her cheeks. "Danooks do not have clothes."

"You're not like them." Tor took off his tunic and motioned for her to stand.

Fuascailt stood tentatively.

Tor slipped his tunic over her head. "Now you have clothes." He smiled and held his arms out to his sides, turning in a circle three times. The rain continued to pour, but they were protected by an invisible shelter. "Let's rest until morning."

***

Tor awoke at the first ray of dawn. Rain still fell softly, but with his loss of concentration during sleep, a few holes appeared in their shelter. He groaned and yawned.

Iontus began to whine. Fuascailt gathered him to her. "He's hungry."

Tor turned his back to the mother and child. "Does he eat solid food yet?"

"Yes, when we have some. I cannot bring myself to kill your kind for food. I have hunted hares and netted fish. He can eat the fish, but most meat is too tough for him. He likes berries, but the Danooks often bar me from searching for them. So, I nurse him."

Tor reached into his pack. "Try this," he said, handing her two pieces of honey bread.

Fuascailt took a bite. "Mmm." She broke off a small piece and gave it to her son. He devoured it and reached for more. Fuascailt laughed.

Tor grinned. *I like that sound.* He bit into a piece of bread and rinsed it down with water, handing the container to Fuascailt. She took the container and imitated what Tor had done, but coughed, being used to lapping water. A second attempt proved more successful.

"We should go," he said.

"You'll really take care of us?"

"Yes."

Tor waved his hands and the rain stopped. They began to walk, Fuascailt carrying the child on her hip. She stopped. "The blood is gone." She looked at Tor's tanned face. "The rain. You made everything clean."

He placed an arm around her shoulders. "Let's go."

Atop the salt dome, Tor summoned rain again. The drops stayed ten steps behind them until they reached Libretante. Once within the walls of the library, the rain came in a deluge.

Fuascailt clutched his arm at the ferocious roar. He took her hand and kissed her fingertips. "To wash away our scents. You're safe now."

14
PATHFINDER

"MAMERE!" Tor called as they entered Libretante.

Illuminet and her daughters rushed from the balconies above at the sound of Tor's voice, Terk leading the way. She stopped stone still. Tae and Illuminet plowed into her back.

Tor felt Fuascailt tremble. He increased the pressure of his semi-embrace. "Mamere, Taekeyla, Terkoyze, this is Fuascailt and her son, Iontus."

"What? Where?" Terk began.

Illuminet stepped forward around her daughters. "Welcome, child," she said. "Don't be afraid." She touched her chest. "I'm Illuminet Ignis, Tor's mother." She gestured with her hand toward her daughters. "These are Tor's sisters." She smiled in their direction. "Terk is a little headstrong, and it would seem that Tae has lost her voice. Come in." She held her arms out for the baby. "I think I can find some of Tor's old clothes to fit your little one, and I'm certain my girls have something they can share with you." She gave them a pointed, rebuking glare.

"Of course," Tae finally said. "Let Mamere hold Iontus and come with us."

The little boy offered no resistance to Illuminet. She turned to the three girls. "Hurry back and we'll have our midday meal." She gazed at Tor. "How long do you plan for the rain to fall upon this parched land? The ground might have a hard time absorbing so much so fast."

"A little longer. To wash away all our scent. We have much to tell. First, I'd like to avail myself of the fresh, clean water and bathe."

"Bathe?" Fuascailt paused in her walk with Tor's sisters.

"Oh, yes," Tae and Terk said together and urged their guest along.

Illuminet jutted her chin toward the area used for bathing, and Tor left.

She smoothed the hair back on the little one's head. "Well, it appears Leviaddan is up to something. Let's get you situated."

Iontus pointed toward where the three girls had gone. "Momomom."

"She'll be right back."

***

Half an hour later, everyone returned to the dining area. Illuminet had set Iontus in a large blocked-off area and given him several wooden toys to play with, but he mainly chewed on them. Illuminet prepared a meal.

Fuascailt wore clothes of the same construct as Tae and Terk. The slightly gray tint to her face was gone, thanks to a bath, and her skin gleamed like porcelain ivory. The girls had braided her long blonde hair, and it shone diamond-like, reflecting light in splashes of color.

Tor returned last, rubbing his chin. "Mamere, I'm needing to shave now."

"Shave?" Fuascailt repeated.

"Cut the hair from my face," he explained.

Her hand instantly flew to her neck.

"Not you," Tae said. "Only men shave."

"My father has long chin hair."

"Not *all* men shave," Illuminet said. She gazed at her son, and a sly smile crept across her lips. "Let's eat. Then, I think there's a long story to tell."

***

Illuminet sat with her hands covering her face. She released a compunctious sigh. "My sweet girl, you have endured far too much." She contemplated Fuascailt.

"So, you are telling me that my father is the cause of all this misery?" She turned her eyes to Tor. "How could you want to save me?"

Illuminet took her hand. "None of this is your fault. You're an innocent."

Fuascailt took a deep breath. "The Wulfgar mate for life, but the Danooks are wild, angry. And humans? Or Nephilim? I know not. I know my father is not to be trusted. What do I do? I have left the only people I've ever known. What if he tracks me?"

Tor murmured, "I know exactly where to hide you, but for now, you should stay with Mamere."

"Will you be where I am hidden?"

"Eventually. And when all is over, you will be free to be wherever you choose." He smiled toward her.

She smiled and the tiny whiskers next to her nose wiggled. "I'll go wherever you go." She looked down. "I mean, if you would have me."

The silence became suffocating.

Illuminet cleared her throat and said, "You are very young for those decisions…"

"No, we're not," Tor interrupted. "But it might be a long time before we can act upon it." He took Fuascailt's hand. "When my father is free, we'll decide what to do then. Right now, I have a quest, and you must remain with Mamere. With the love and loyalty we share, there is no obstacle too big to overcome.

"Mamere, bring on the scrolls. We must find how to get to Sliabh Aer. I'm convinced that's where we'll find Iolar Mór Bán."

***

Each triplet and Illuminet took up a scroll. Fuascailt looked on, bewildered. She carefully touched one of the yellowed parchments. "These markings are words? You *read* them?"

"Yes," Tor responded. "While we're away, Mamere can teach you to read, and then you can help research Terk's mission." He glanced toward Tae. "I'm certain Tae's endeavor is last for the complexity of it."

Fuascailt flattened a small scroll, no wider than the length of an index finger and about as long as a forearm. "This one is different," she said. "It's drawings. Even Danooks have drawings."

"Let me see," Illuminet said. She moved beside Fuascailt. "How did I miss this?"

"It's very small, Mamere," Tae said, joining her mother.

Tor and Terk came to the other side of Illuminet and Fuascailt. Tor ran his teeth over his bottom lip several times, deep in thought. "It's not done. We have only a portion of a map. This shows the far side of a mountain."

Iontus repeatedly slapped Tor's hand as he placed a finger on one spot of the drawing. Touching a place on the parchment, brought a loud squeal from the child.

Tor arched an eyebrow. He continued, "This oval swirl must be a wicket to another world. Iolar Mór Bán will be on the other side. We need the rest of the map."

Iontus gusted a breath. Tor stared into the little boy's eyes a long time, feeling a strange connection.

"Yes," Illuminet concurred. "Spread out and search for other scrolls this size. I'm sure we overlooked this because it's tiny." She turned to Fuascailt. "Did you find this?"

"No. Iontus handed it to me."

"Ah," Tor murmured and gave Iontus a smile.

Illuminet nodded and nudged her shoulder. "Take him with you."

Fuascailt took her son's hand, and everyone began a search for small scrolls.

After several minutes, Iontus tugged his mother's hand and lifted another small scroll. Fuascailt took it. "Where did you find this?"

The little boy pulled her along and pointed underneath the wall of cubbyholes to a space about three inches off the floor.

"Of course!" Fuascailt called, "Under the shelf. On the floor."

Everyone dropped to hands and knees, even flat on their bellies, to peer into the dark recess. Each began to rake hands under the wall of cubbyholes. Eleven more small scrolls were recovered.

"Either they fell or were deliberately hidden." Illuminet unrolled and placed the scrolls together like a jigsaw puzzle until a map appeared.

"Here we are!" Tor cried, pointing to a square labeled Libretante. "The trail ends at a wicket," he continued.

"That will be a long walk," Terk grumbled.

"Maybe I can speed us up with some wind," Tor boasted.

"Not wise," Tae said. "Leviaddan might detect your use of your powers. So, we need to get packing and moving."

Fuascailt's hand covered Tor's. "Avoid my father if you can."

A bit disappointed, mouth frowning, Tor nodded agreement.

15

TREK

FOR the next several days, the teens gathered food and other supplies for a long journey while Illuminet worked to stitch thirteen scrolls together in a way that they could be fan-folded in Tor's pack. She flattened them and held them down with flat stones, frequently stopping to play for short periods with an active little boy, who would sometimes sit on the low table and shake his head while pointing at a place that either required a stitch or needed a stich removed. Illuminet learned to trust the child's instincts. His silent suggestions proved to be correct. She still could not believe she was about to be responsible for Leviaddan's offspring.

Illuminet watched Fuascailt with Tor. *The girl's heart is pure.* How she could be so untainted still puzzled Illuminet, and Iontus was an absolute delight. Somehow qualities from Fayla, Leviaddan's mother, must have passed to them.

Compassion. I told Tor it would profit him loyalty—but this is devotion. Fuascailt ran her fingers through Tor's waist-length hair.

Illuminet's heart skipped a beat. *More! She loves him. He rescued her, and she is his forever.*

Illuminet watched Tor squeeze Fuascailt's hand. *And he loves her! My children are no longer children.*

Fuascailt worked until her fingers bled weaving hemp into rope. Tae and Terk laughed with her, bonding.

Iontus ran underfoot, knowing he would receive attention. But the little boy craved hugs and being lifted into the air by Tor.

Illuminet put her hand to her mouth. *They were rejected by both Danooks and humans. The only reason the Danooks let them live was fear of Leviaddan. And the humans would have slaughtered them if Tor hadn't been there. And they found the map. Leviaddan will kill them himself if he doesn't believe they're dead. He has to think they're dead!*

She put her arm around Fuascailt. "I need some of your blood and some of Iontus's blood."

"Why?"

"Leviaddan has to believe you died in the raid on Danooks." She picked up the little boy and cuddled him. "I'm sorry, but it will hurt."

"How much?" Fuascailt asked, her voice hitching.

Illuminet lifted one end of a small scroll they had removed to put the map together. "One of these for each of you should do."

Fuascailt looked at Tor, her blue eyes blinking back tears. He nodded, but with a look of consternation on his face.

She left with Illuminet. A few minutes later, Iontus screamed. They returned with bandaged hands and the baby reaching for Tor. He took him and soothed him the best he could.

Illuminet held up her two makeshift vials. "Give him to his mother. You need to go spread the blood."

"Now?" Tor arched an eyebrow.

"I feel an urgency. Do it."

Tor handed Iontus to Fuascailt, snagged a small pack, and headed out.

***

Early the next morning, Illuminet awoke to the sound of someone retching. "Did you travel nonstop?" she asked when she saw her son.

"Yes," Tor gasped between heaves.

"What's wrong?"

"There must have been another raid. It was a massacre, though the Danooks must have fought back. Bodies littered the vale. The stench!" He vomited again into the latrine.

"Did you get the blood done?"

"Yes. I put it close together near some badly decaying bodies."

"I hope it works."

***

At the end of the week, the triplets prepared to leave. Helping to adjust straps, Illuminet said, "These packs will be heavy."

"We'll be fine, Mamere," Tae assured.

Terk said, "I added more vines and littered the ground with thorns and thistles."

"We need to go," Tor said.

Fuascailt sniffled.

Iontus clung to Tor's neck and then buried his face against his mother's chest.

Tor kissed Fuascailt full on the mouth. Then he hugged his mother.

Tae and Terk gave hugs all around, and the triplets headed for the door.

Illuminet realized the four months of preparation had changed all of them, and the only child in their company was Iontus.

"Be careful," she said.

"We'll see you soon," Tor said with a confidence Illuminet had only seen in Yarwhin. She kissed her son's cheek once more, and the triplets stepped into the fast-approaching dawn.

***

As the triplets neared the salt dome, Terk grumbled, "It's hotter than the fires of Lavan."

"I can't help that," Tor said. "Mamere made me put blood out because she's afraid Leviaddan will come. He'd surely detect use of our powers."

As he spoke, they heard a scream that shook the ground.

"By the gods!" Tae said under her breath.

Tor put a finger to his lips. They stealthily climbed the mound, using the spikes Tor had left from before. Just below the apex, they flattened themselves against the briny sand and peered over the top.

Below, a being a large as their father flung the remains of the dead in all directions. Yarwhin had not described his brother except that he had wings. Leviaddan appeared to be split down the middle, one side as black as Yarwhin's obsidian walls—hair, skin, wing; the other half, chalky white. The eye on his black side gleamed red, while the other one was crystal blue, just like Fuascailt's. He was human in features, but Tor understood why he was feared. Yarwhin at least appeared to be a giant man. Leviaddan was other-worldly.

Leviaddan sniffed the ground and, again, tossed body parts and bellowed. "You will pay!" he roared and took flight.

The triplets burrowed into any loose salt to cover themselves.

Leviaddan circled six times and then flew the direction they would need to travel.

"By the gods!" muttered Tor. "If he saw us, he might be lying in wait." He looked back. "At least he didn't go toward Mamere."

"Or Fauscailt," Tae said with a grin.

"Yes." Tor nodded. "He must think them dead."

"That's good, right?" asked Terk.

"Yes, for them. But that maniac might go after all humans, maybe Danooks too." Tor hoisted his pack. "Let's get as far as we can."

Before they could begin their descent, fire rained onto the dead bodies. Smoke billowed upward. The stink of burning flesh filled the triplets' nostrils.

Leviaddan made another sweep and then headed in a ninety-degree direction.

"He went a different way," Terk said.

"He's going as far as he thinks the marauders could have gotten—each direction." Tor looked back toward Libretante.

"I've camouflaged them well," Terk said. "Yggamay's children have the library covered. And the flowers they are putting out will mask any other scent."

"Okay." He bit his lip.

Tae touched his arm. "You have a mission. Let's go."

Tor nodded, and they slid down the dome, quickening their pace the second their feet touch the flat of the vale.

In a trot, they came upon group after group of charred nomads.

"By the gods!" Terk muttered.

"He's seeking revenge on any who would have been close enough to have been responsible for the raids," Tor surmised. "Let's keep moving."

After two more hours, they stopped seeing Leviaddan's carnage, and the sun began to set. They made camp, but none had an appetite after the gore they had seen. They slept fitfully, their dreams filled with smoke and blood.

Through desert, over rocky, hilly terrains day after day, they walked, finally coming to a vast plain covered with green grass dotted with wildflowers. A wide river meandered through it. A mountain was visible in the distance.

Tae asked, "Is that Sliabh Aer?"

"No," Tor sighed.

"No," Terk affirmed. "Sliabh Aer will be on the other side of the wicket."

"At least two more weeks," Tor said, letting his pack slide to the ground. "And then the real unknown."

"Let's get closer to the river," Tae suggested.

"Tomorrow," Tor said. "We'll camp on the banks." He surveyed the sky. "Not enough daylight left to get there."

Terk said, "I don't see any place for Danooks to hide."

"I'm sure Leviaddan might have other tricks, and we'd be too open." Tor put his hand against a stone mound. "At least here, we'll be camouflaged a bit."

That night, they heard groans and soughing through tree boughs accompanied by loud plops as if something heavy fell to the ground. Looking out the opening to their pop-bubble served little purpose. Not a single star twinkled, but the sky was obsidian black, without even a haloed moon of an eclipse.

Tor sighed. "I fear what we'll find in the morning."

16
AIN'T NO MOUNTAIN HIGH ENOUGH

TOR'S fear was confirmed by day. If Leviaddan himself had not been there, he had left in place traps for any seeking the wicket to Iolar Mór Bán. As far as the eye could see, gargantuan gargoyles garrisoned the river, each a replication of Leviaddan.

"He will always send his minions," Tor mumbled.

"What?" Terk asked

"That's what Mamere said," Tae replied.

"Let's see what they've got," Tor said, defiantly.

Nothing happened for the first mile. One more step brought the gargoyles hurling stones, which they created out of air, the size of pop-bubbles. The triplets retreated, and the gargoyles returned to stationary.

"If one of those hits us, we'll be flattened," Tae said.

"True," Tor said. He wrinkled his brow. "They're stone. Can you pulverize them?" he asked, turning to Terk.

"I can try." She rubbed her chin. "Or maybe bind them."

"A bog!" Tae shouted. "I can make them sink into mud."

"Good deal," Tor said. "Get busy. While you two work your magic, I'll conjure a wind to knock some over."

Terk chanted, "Climb, bind, hold them fast." Thick vines sprouted and snaked their way around some of the gargoyles. They broke through the first few, but Terk added power to her voice, and the plants strengthened.

Tae voiced, "Muck to suck and get stuck."

Almost laughing at the words she chose, Tor quieted as gooey puddles formed around the feet of the living statues, and they slowly began to sink up to their necks, immobilized, although it took all day.

Tor chose his own thoughts. "Fly away, fly away home. Go back to where you belong." Multiple funnels formed, lifting some of the giant stone creatures into the clouds where bright flashes and crackling sent bits of rock hailing back to the ground.

He pointed. "Terk, gather a few of those. I think you might need them on your quest."

A full day of intensive concentration ridded the area of Leviaddan's first obstacle. They slept again, drained by the exertion and left at first light on a narrow path that had dried in Tae's sludge.

They looked back once they passed the creatures. Some still struggled to free themselves from bindings or bogs.

The three plodded on.

***

Near dark, the triplets made camp a hundred yards from the river.

"A dip would be so refreshing," Terk said, looking longingly toward the slow-moving, clear water.

"Too dangerous," Tor said. "I'll make you your very own little rain cloud on the opposite side of the pop-bubble entrance." He smiled. "After all, you did great work with those gargoyles, and once you're done, Tae and I can have a turn."

Terk stuck her tongue out at her brother but accepted his gift.

Once all were washed, Tae said, "Do we dare try for fish?"

Tor shook his head. "As calm as the water appears, I'd bet it would spawn flesh-eating rhiamas."

"I guess it's dried ox tails and"—She plucked a piece of vegetation—"dandelion greens."

"I'm hungry enough to eat the whole ox," Terk said, and her stomach rumbled in agreement.

They all laughed and set about making a small supper.

The soft gurgling of the river lulled the triplets to sleep. Finally, Tae roused, stretched, yawned. Opening her eyes, she bolted upright. "Wake up!"

"What's wrong?" Tor asked.

"How long did we sleep?"

Terk grunted and rolled over. Tae shook her sister. "We've slept forever." She pointed at Tor. "Feel your chin."

Tor put his hand to his face. "By the gods!" He had a full, if patchy, beard.

Terk finally sat up and rubbed sleep from her eyes. She let out a little scream. "Who is that?"

"Our brother!" Tae snapped. She stepped outside the pop-bubble.

The river still meandered along lazily. Nothing seemed out of place from when they went to bed, yet something had to have changed.

Tor came out. "Tae, Terk wants you. She says it's gravely important, but I have to stay out here."

Tae went back inside to see Terk's eyes stretched wide. "I've gone through at least one woman cycle. Have you?" Terk pushed back her blanket. Her whole pallet and garment were covered in dried blood.

Tae checked herself and her bed, which also was covered, though not as heavily as her sister's. "My flow has never been as heavy as yours, but, yes, it appears I did also. Did we sleep nearly a month?

"Maybe. We need to get cleaned up and get away from here." She pointed outside. "I think the river sang us to sleep."

Gathering their soiled clothing and bedding, Tae and Terk stepped outside. Terk said curtly without a glance at her brother, "Tor, we need a rain shower, and I mean now."

"By the gods!" Tae shouted.

Terk turned.

Tor swayed like a sapling in a stiff wind, sound asleep on his feet.

Tae rushed to him and shook him. "Wake up, Tor!"

"Hm?" He forced his eyes open.

Terk repeated, "Make it rain now!"

He held his hands out, and a drizzle started.

"He's too out of it," Tae said, and she began a circle in the sand. Water rose into the trench she made. After nearly an hour, a geyser shot upward, drenching all three.

The cool, clean water cleared their senses. Terk and Tae washed the laundry and spread the bedding on the ground to dry. Tae spoke the word, "Calm," repeatedly until spray subsided.

"We have to get away from this river," Tae said. "Leviaddan has poisoned it."

"Swim?" Tor asked.

"I don't think so," Tae said. She threw a piece of jerky into the river. Within seconds, the shimmer that had caused the water to look so clear joined to form skeletal fish with razor sharp teeth. "Rhiamas."

"By the gods!" Terk growled. She began to mound and pat dirt. The mound elongated and widened. An hour later, an earthen bridge spanned the river. "Let's go!" she shouted, grabbing her pack.

Tae followed, and Tor brought up the rear.

The second Terk's foot touched the center of the bridge, a tentacle shot from the water and wrapped around her ankle, jerking her over the side. She dug into the dirt to keep from being pulled into the current.

"Terk!" Tae shrieked and clutched her sister's hand.

Another tentacle erupted with a shower of water and grasped Tae's wrist.

Tor charged with his broadsword, chopping both tentacles.

A massive gray-green head with huge diamond shaped orange eyes emerged from the water.

The detached tentacles wiggled toward the head.

"Tor!" Terk cried. "Freeze the water."

He blew, and his breath became ice crystals. A frozen film covered the river.

"Don't stop," Tae said, and she and Terk scrambled back to the top of the dirt dam.

Into the next morning, he continued puffing a stream of wind until the water no longer moved, and solid ice three feet deep appeared.

"Run!" He commanded. "I'm not sure how long this will hold."

His sisters wasted no time obeying. As his own feet landed with a jump on the far side, the ice cracked. Tentacles burst through the fissure.

"Keep going!" Tor bellowed.

When they lost sight of the river, they collapsed.

"By the gods!" wheezed out in a chorus from all three.

Tor stared toward the mountain in the distance. "Another week."

"And then we climb," Terk said.

"But now we rest." Tae lay where she had fallen.

***

A change in the wind...An odd sound...An unusual smell. The triplets stayed alert, slept little, traveled until they had to stop.

"This is too easy," Terk whispered one night around the campfire.

"We haven't started up the mountain yet," Tae said. "So far, we've battled, Terra-Firma and Water. Fire and Wind haven't shown up yet."

"They will," Tor said, and then he went to bed.

He had hardly closed his eyes when Tae shook him. "Tor, wake up. Fire has reared its head."

"What?" He stumbled outside the pop-bubble with his sister where Terk stared into the distance at an orange glow on the horizon.

She turned. "It looks like a blaze around the base of the mountain."

"Too easy…" Tor thought aloud.

"Easy?" Terk asked.

"A hard rain can douse a fire." He began to pack. "Let's go."

"In the dark?" Tae asked.

"It would be unexpected."

The sisters followed Tor's example. Laden with the dwindling supplies, they picked their way across the plain toward the glow.

Drawing close, they stopped and covered their noses. "This fire is not natural. Oh! The brimstone stench!" Tor gagged. "This smells just like when Leviaddan burned those bodies." He froze. "It's more bodies!"

He broke into a full run, calling down rain as he ran. Tae and Terk trailed behind him. By the time they reached the ring of fire, it had become a smoldering fog.

Tor fell to his knees. Tae and Terk jerked him up. "You can't stop now," Tae said. "That's what he wants."

"Damn him to everlasting torment!" Terk growled

Tor looked up. "We're here, and the sun's coming up." He looked skyward. The top of a huge mountain rose above the clouds. He pulled climbing spikes and rope from his pack. "Time to climb." He vaulted over the river of carnage.

***

Foot by foot they ascended. Near the bottom, they used the trees to keep balance. Once the trees thinned, they utilized spikes. The temperature dropped. It became harder to breathe. Intermittent clouds left icy dew on their skin. They came to a landing, and before them swirled a mist, much like the one in the overhang in Yarwhin's prison.

Tor started through, but his sisters pulled him back.

"Rest tonight. Eat. We need our strength," Tae said.

"And," Terk added, "we must enter as one."

17
BATTLE OF CARRION TUIRLINGTHE

TAE shivered from the high mountain air and a coat of fresh snow on the ground. "Tor, can you warm the air?" she asked, teeth chattering.

He made a supplication for warmer air, but nothing happened. He furrowed his brow. "Tae, make a small pond of fresh water. Terk, put up a stone barricade to keep anyone else from getting to us."

Both sisters tried their special gift to naught.

"As I thought," Tor said. "Somehow our powers are nullified here."

"Does that mean Leviaddan's are also?" Tae asked.

"I think so," Tor replied. "That's why the climb offered no resistance except for the mountain itself."

"Good," Terk said. "We can eat and sleep tonight without fear." She turned to the wicket. "Then, tomorrow we go to another world."

They pitched the pop-bubble. Tor looked around. "There's nothing to use to start a fire."

Tae opened her pack. "Very little food left. I sure hope we can resupply over there."

Terk shrugged. "What's one more cold meal? And I guess we'll have to huddle together for warmth." She grinned. "I claim center for the first two hours."

They ate and turned in.

***

When morning arrived, one step into the frosty air caused the triplets to be wide awake. They ate the last of their hardtack bread and packed up.

They clasped hands. "Just like when we left Papere," Tor said. "But be ready to use a weapon or your Elemental as soon as we cross over."

They stepped into the wicket and felt as if they were spiraling head-over-heels, and they worried they would lose the little bit of breakfast they had eaten. And it grew colder and colder.

They saw light, but hurricane-force winds kept pushing them back.

"Tor! Do something!" Tae shouted over the roaring wind.

Tor chanted, "Gentle breeze…gentle breeze…gentle breeze."

After what seemed an eternity, a small hole appeared in the center of the barrier.

Tor chanted.

The hole grew.

Tor chanted.

The hole expanded to a size the teens could run through if they bent over. They took their opportunity.

The wicket spat them out with force. They landed in a snowbank taller than they were. And more snow fell in giant flakes, so thick they had trouble seeing one another.

Without warning, Tor yelped in pain. Tae crawled to the sound of his voice. An ice arrow had pierced his right shoulder. Blood froze around the wound.

"Terk!" Tae shouted.

"Coming!"

"Tor's been hit. Can you get us some cover? As near as I can tell, we're wide open. This is a plain, flat, no trees."

"I think I see hills in the distance. I'll try to pull stones."

She reached forward and pulled. No stones fell, but an avalanche cascaded down the mountain in the distance.

Tae made water trickle over the arrow, trying to keep the water warm enough to melt the ice.

Terk knelt beside her siblings. "Who shot the arrow?" She looked around and strained her ears.

Dead silence was shattered by a sound of rolling thunder shaking the ground.

Tor groaned and sat up. "I don't know if our powers can defeat what's coming. Nock some arrows. Load some stones." He drew his sword.

"Are you able to fight?" Tae clutched his arm.

Terk laid her hand on the wound. "Papere said I could heal."

Warmth spread through Tor's body, and he stood.

The rumbling increased in volume and intensity. Emerging from the swirling snow, hundreds of horsenae, composed of eddying wind, mounted by ice warriors armed with ice weapons, charged toward the triplets.

"We have to shoot for the riders!" Tor shouted over the tumult. "Fire!"

Tae and Terk released arrows and stones. The arrows bounced off the frozen enemy. Terk's stones cracked the ice.

"My arrows are useless!" Tae shrieked. "A river! It will at least slow them."

"My rocks are only chipping or cracking them," Terk said. She picked up a piece of a gargoyle. "I'll try these."

"Keep firing," Tor told her. "Once Tae gets a good river, add dirt. Make it a bog. If the horsenae can't move, we can attack the riders."

Tae moved her hands in a flowing motion, calling upon the Water Elemental.

Terk loaded her sling with bits of gargoyle and pelted the riders. Some lost limbs. Others cracked down the middle after numerous hits.

Tor grasped his javelin but thought better. Letting go, he mimed throwing, and lightning bolts left his hands. The first pierced the chest of the lead rider; the second, the eye socket of the rider next to him.

Still, the army plunged forward.

A twenty-foot-wide shallow river began to flow between the oncoming army and the triplets after an incomputable amount of time. Tae mumbled, "I feel as if my arms are going to fall off." She continued calling forth water. "Terk, add some dirt," she said.

Terk shifted her attention from slinging stones to pulling dirt from beneath the snow after she massaged her own shoulder that throbbed from repeated movements.

After shaking feeling back into his hands, Tor hurled a barrage of lightning bolts with both hands.

The river became a slow-moving sludge. When the horsenae stepped into it, they became stuck, unable to free their feet, though they struggled to do so.

Riders dismounted. Horsenae behind the front line collided with the stuck line. Riders fell off.

Tor pulled his sword and charged into the throng, his feet moving like wind and never touching the ground. The power and speed of Wind behind each swing, he rent the ice warriors in two until only a handful were left.

On the other side of the river, Tor stood his ground. The final dozen marched onward, intent on destruction.

"Stop!" Tor shouted. "Who sent you?"

The line halted. The center warrior spoke in a voice that sounded like a howling storm. "We serve our master to the end."

Tae and Terk covered their ears at the sound of the voice.

"Who is your master?" Tor demanded.

"Leviaddan."

"Are there more of you?"

"At the base of the mountain, we stop, but we were called forth to eliminate the intruders."

"And you will not stop?"

"No!" With that, the final wave charged Tor.

With a yell, he spun, sword outward, faster and faster, until he became a cyclone. The sound of the warriors breaking apart clinked like ice in a glass.

Then all was silence.

Toward them rode one last being, but she was mounted on a great ursine, hairy beast of a grayish hue. She herself was encompassed by shimmering white furs, though her skin shone with a pale-blue tone. She stopped and surveyed the battlefield. "I am Chriostalach Börgin, Guardian of the Wicket to Örnland."

Tor held his sword ready. "Did Leviaddan send you?"

Her roar sounded like rain pouring. "No!" She waved a hand. "His creatures overwhelmed me when he could not corrupt me to allow him passage. I was forced to retreat up the mountain. I've waited and prayed for the one who could vanquish his horde. I did not expect children."

Tor dipped his head and introduced them. "We are not children. We are the Elementals reborn. We are on a quest to see Iolar Mór Bán."

"I can only grant you passage through the wicket. You are free to seek the Great White Eagle. I can neither hinder you nor help you."

"Will he see us?"

"*She* is in great turmoil. I cannot say, but I will send word of your victory here today at Carrion Tuirlingthe."

She raised her arm, and an over-large raven landed on her forearm. She spoke in chirps and caws, sending the bird on its way.

"You must be exhausted," she said, turning back to the triplets. "Rest and refresh in my camp tonight. You may begin your climb to Sliabh Aer tomorrow." She turned and headed away.

Tor, Tae, and Terk had no choice but to follow.

18
HEAD IN THE CLOUDS

HIGH-PITCHED, cheerful flute music was the first thing the triplets heard to indicate a camp. The snow still fell thick, and a kind of fog limited vision. At last, a wall of tight-packed snow came into view. The wall extended into a large dome, speckled with chimneys emitting a soft-gray smoke. The aromas of pan-seared fish and sautéed onions caused their mouths to water and their stomachs to rumble.

Chriostalach dismounted her steed, and several more beings, looking much like her, rushed forward to care for the animal. She threw back her hood to reveal silvery-white hair and pointed ears. Her lavender eyes glistened. All the other beings had similar coloring, varying only in shade. Both males and female appeared not to cut their hair.

"What are you?" Terk asked without thinking.

Chriostalach laughed. "We are Winter Elves. Each wicket is guarded by some kind of Elf."

"Mamere did not report a guardian on Lavan," Tae murmured.

"Yes, Lavan." Chriostalach folded her arms across an ample bosom with a garment that showed cleavage. "Not all Elves remain pure in spirit. Those who are corrupted are called Drows."

"That's what Papere said," Terk blurted.

Chriostalach arched an eyebrow.

Tae elbowed her sister and scowled at her.

The Elf covered her mouth to hide a smirk. "The Guardian of Lavan gave in to greed; thus, no guardian. Guardians are given the color to blend with their environment. Lavan's Guardian should have been a fluctuation of the colors of fire. No doubt, he appeared leathery black. If I had succumbed, I would be translucent white." She beckoned with her hand. "Now, come."

They entered a smaller structure like the large one. A fire burned in the center, and the temperature was comfortable if clothed warmly.

Chriostalach stroked her chin. "You will need better clothing if you are to visit Iolar Mór Bán.

"Is that helping?" Tor asked, tilting his head to the side.

"No. That is supplying." Without further comment, their hostess gave a firm clap, and servants brought food and drink.

After the meal, the triplets were shown to a room with a hot spring for bathing, and then they were given heavy woolen garments, much like the outfit Chriostalach wore. Where her neckline plunged, Tae's and Terk's had rounded necks, and Tor's was square. All of them had wool breeches and socks and leather boots. Amazingly, the clothes fit.

They returned to the area where they had eaten seated on furs. Their hostess was not present. A smaller female, dressed more conservatively, approached them. "My mistress has prepared you quarters. You are instructed to stay as long as you need before continuing your quest." She showed them a room where three fur pallets awaited. "Rest now and join my mistress tomorrow for breakfast."

"It appears to still be light," Tor said.

"Yes. We are in our summer season. There is no darkness. Winter brings no light. Be glad you did not come in winter. To climb in darkness would mean death." She handed them three eye masks. "You might need these to sleep." She left without further comment.

They each claimed a bed, Tor in the center. They sat on his bed and talked a bit. "She can't help?" Terk asked.

"But she is," Tae countered.

Tor twisted his lips to the side. "Perhaps she means hands-on help, like guiding us or climbing with us. I'll take provisions and supplies."

Terk scratched her head. "She could not defeat Leviaddan's horde, yet they could not enter here and overrun her."

"I don't understand all of it," Tor said. "At least she seems to be on our side."

"Let's hope it's not an act," Terk grunted.

"It's not. She has true hatred for our uncle," Tae said.

"Spurned?" Terk gave a sardonic grin.

"Who knows?" Tae shrugged one shoulder. "Let's rest and talk to the people. They might let something slip."

Tor rubbed his shoulder where the ice arrow had struck. "I *am* tired and sore."

Terk rubbed her temples discreetly. *I can't let him know how tired healing him made me. He'd never let me do it again, and Papere thinks that might be my biggest strength in our fight.* She said, "It's been a long day…week?"

"I don't know either," Tor said.

His sisters moved to their pallets. With masks over their eyes, they were asleep within minutes.

***

Chriostalach greeted her guests the next morning with a cheerful smile. Breakfast was spread before them, items they had never seen. Their hostess's melodic voice said, "Snowberries with yak cream, hominy porridge, and malted slush."

The triplets took note that all the foods they had eaten since arrival had a whitish color, though tasty.

Chriostalach began, "After consulting the spirit guides, I think it best for you to leave today. I've provided packs, provisions, proper clothing, and climbing gear."

"Is there a guide?" Tor ventured.

"No. I've given all I can. The rest is up to you." She stood. "Now, I must walk among my people and see to posting new sentries at the wicket." She left.

"Well," Tae muttered, "she could use lessons in politeness."

"I wouldn't suggest it," Tor said. "Eat up and let's get going."

"We didn't get to see the town," Terk said.

"And we won't," Tor said. "I think our conversation was overheard last night." He jerked his head toward the door. "Maybe their ears give them sharper hearing."

"We meant no harm" Tae said.

"And she knows that," Tor acknowledged, "or we would be dead."

They finished breakfast, refreshed themselves, and gathered supplies.

Chriostalach waited for them at the entrance to her compound. "Safe journey," she bade them. "Stay vigilant."

In addition to the supplies, she handed Tae a quiver filled with ice arrows and Terk a bag of ice shards. Nodding to Tor, she said, "Your lightning bolts serve you well." She turned, and two sentries took their positions at the entrance.

With a knitted brow, Tae mused, "How is it we speak the same language?"

Terk sighed. "My guess is Gran Sabita. And I bet we will be able to understand others as well."

"I did feel my ears burning and my throat constricting when we stepped into the mist." Tor nodded. "Still, I think that will be one of your gifts, Terk. Gran Sabita gave it to us this time because she knew that you had not mastered your Elemental."

Terk grinned. "I'll gladly accept her gift."

***

Tor hoisted the heaviest pack, and his sisters took up the other two. They walked toward the base of the mountain. A full day's travel brought them to a circle of ice crystals, which encompassed the area around Chriostalach's camp.

Tor held up his hand to stop his sisters. "Be prepared for anything once we cross this barrier."

Tae let her pack slide to the ground. "We've walked all day with only brief stops for food and drink. I suggest we camp inside tonight and brave whatever lies beyond tomorrow."

"Good idea," said Terk, letting her pack hit the ground.

Tor frowned, thinking of all the daylight they had, but he soon saw the wisdom in rest.

Tae laughed when she reached into her pack and pulled out a mask. "She knew we'd need darkness."

Terk retrieved a canister from her pack and opened it. They had snacked on dried fruit for most of the day. A note said:

Heat the canister over a fire. The inside will make a hearty soup, and you can eat the container afterward.

"Fascinating," she muttered. Each one of them had half a dozen such containers.

They pitched their pop-bubble, started a fire with flint and stone and a wad of hair provided in abundance, ate, and fell asleep.

***

Next morning, they ate a quick breakfast of dried fruit and a kind of sweet-tasting bread. Packed and ready to travel, Tor warned again to be prepared for anything once they crossed the plane where the strange ice circle lay.

In case they be thrown to different places, the teens clasped hands and stepped through the ice circle. It felt as if a cold blade slid through them, yet they were unharmed as their feet touched the other side—a side with patches of grass intermingled with melting snow and ice. Gardens of all kind dotted around the protective circle.

Huts with a few Elves were scattered for about a hundred yards.

"Well, now we know where their food comes from," Terk said.

None of the inhabitants paid any attention to the triplets.

Though still cold, the air was not frigid, and the heavy cloaks Chriostalach had given them became too warm. Just the wool tunics and breeches were enough. They tied the cloaks to their packs because outside the circle, they realized the sun did rise and set, just not all the way to darkness. When it was overhead, the temperature moderated.

Another day's journey finally brought them to the base of the mountain and a heavy tree line. Looking beyond, showed a natural progression— thinning trees, mostly evergreens; barren rock face; clouds obscuring the summit.

"We're looking at three or four days more, at least," Tor said. Let's make camp against the tree line and venture in tomorrow. The gods alone know what might be in there."

***

As the triplets began their hike through a forest, Terk stopped to touch trees, seeking their guidance and safe passage. As she ran her hand along the trunk of a towering pine, she gasped and jerked her hand back.

"What's wrong?" Tor asked.

"This one is Yggadon. He said to stay vigilant and keep our eyes peeled for Yetis. He warned against killing them and suggests offering a bribe for passage."

"What kind of bribe? What's a Yeti? What would it want?" Tor blinked in confusion.

"It's a large hairy creature that walks upright. They are powerful, but solitary. They have been known to kill with one blow. And they crave—honey." Terk interpreted what Yggadon told her.

"Honey?" Tae said. "Have you seen any bees? Where would we find honey?"

Terk caressed the tree again, and it soughed, boughs waving slowly. "Looook foooor falllleeeeen treeees,"

"I heard that!" Tor cried. "Thank you, Yggadon."

The tree gave a stiff bow, and the triplets stepped once again into the unknown.

*****

There seemed to be no definite trail, so Tor took the lead and chose what looked like the most direct path.

Two hours in, Terk pointed. "There!"

Three large tree trunks lay prone on the forest floor. Bees buzzed in and out.

Tor bit his lip. "Um, Terk…"

She rolled her eyes. "Let me guess. Since I'm the Terra-Firma Elemental, I should get the honey. Besides, you're afraid of getting stung."

"Well, yeah." He nodded.

"Do we have a container?" Terk asked.

Tae found an empty water skin and cut the top off for a larger hole. "I think this will work."

Making buzzing sounds and barely parting her lips, Terk took the makeshift jar and approached the hive. Bees swarmed her. She inched her hand inside an opening, grasped a piece of honeycomb, and transferred it to the water skin. Honey pooled at the bottom.

She carefully crept away from the hive. When she was far enough away to be unable to reach the fallen log, the bees left her and returned to the hive.

Then, she sprinted to her siblings. She tied off the top and thrust the precious honey at Tor. "They agreed to one piece of comb with honey *if* you make sure Leviaddan never returns here."

"Returns?" Tae cocked an eyebrow.

"Apparently, he's done something to anger Iolar Mór Bán." Terk let out a long breath.

"How can I guarantee their request?" Tor whispered.

"I told them about our quests. They have hope now, just as Papere. Let's move on."

They trekked deeper into woods. Light barely filtered through tree branches, which cast spooky shadows on the ground, and temperatures plummeted, urging the triplets to don the furs they had been given. They were forced to cut briars and vines from around their feet, which made Terk cringe, but she understood the necessity.

They came into a clearing, completely encircled by tall, spindly pines.

"I guess this is as good a place to rest as any," said Tor.

As they let their packs drop, loud snarling, snorting sounds erupted in front of them. Two pines broke under pressure and crashed toward them. A ten-foot simian with a human face charged their direction.

Tae screamed.

Tor stood in front of his sisters.

Terk fumbled with the packs to find the honey.

"Hurry!" Tor shouted as he ducked a blow from a fist the size of a frying pan.

Terk shoved the honey into her brother's hand.

He held it up.

The Yeti stopped its rampage and sniffed. It grabbed the offering and pulled out the comb with thumb and forefinger, licking it clean before chomping it.

"Yes, well," Tor stammered, "we'll just leave you to your snack."

The triplets snatched their packs and raced across the clearing into more woods. They did not stop to rest until they cleared the forest.

When the trees thinned, they dropped, adrenaline spent.

"Diplomacy?" Terk sputtered. "Was that diplomacy?"

"Of a sort," Tae said through gasps for breath.

Tor handed them a water skin and finished it off when it got back to him.

***

They made camp but awoke eager to go on. They scoured the next area with their eyes and strained their ears for any strange sounds.

"It gets steep quick, so get ready to climb," Tor said.

Preparing to travel and climb, rustling and wailing behind them caused all three to draw weapons.

At the edge of the tree line, the Yeti stood, eyes darting all about.

"It's afraid to come into the open," Tor whispered. He gave Terk a little push. "Go talk to it."

"What?"

"You talk to trees and bees. Why not this creature?"

"I don't have any more honey." She glared at her brother and then her sister. "Tae, nock an arrow just in case."

Terk walked slowly toward the Yeti and stopped a few feet in front.

Tor and Tae heard grunting and a high-pitched wail.

Then, the Yeti dipped its head. Terk bowed back, and the creature disappeared into the thicket.

Terk came back to her siblings. "His name is Goliab. He warns that although we may not see foes right now, beware the Banshee. We need to cover our ears with the muffs Chriostalach provided. Goliab says there is no negotiating with a Banshee—shoot to kill. If she gets close enough to kiss you, you're dead."

"Great," Tor groaned. "Where do they hide? How are we supposed to fend off some creature as we climb?"

Tae suggested, "Maybe you can put an umbrella over us, like the one you did with Fuascailt."

"I'll try."

They muffed their ears and began another leg of their journey. Tor created a dome over them and sought the protection of the gods.

The gradual incline grew steeper, and trees to grasp for leverage became sparse. Tor, in the lead, took out climbing hammers and rope but called for a break before continuing. They had to lean into the rock face to keep from slipping backward.

Breather over, Tor plunged ahead. The first spike into the mountain was accompanied by the first scream. Even through the muffs, the sound hurt their ears.

Phantasms with large, gaping mouths oozed from beneath rocks and assailed the three.

Tor, flat on his back with Tae and Terk, one on either side of him, began a barrage of fire, Tor with his lightning bolts, and his sisters with the weapons Chriostalach had bestowed upon them.

"Banshee?" Tor bellowed. "I expected one."

For each creature they felled, another swooped closer and closer. Tae threw her hands in front of her face as one got within inches of her.

"Enough!" Tor roared.

Though dozens of Banshees lay dead, more kept coming. Tor drew in a breath and blew, turning his head side-to-side.

The remaining Banshees cartwheeled through the air.

"Climb!" he shouted.

The triplets scaled the mountain at a furious pace. Periodically, Tor blew Banshees down the slope.

Muscles aching, breathing hard, the teens climbed and popped through fluffy clouds. They watched as the Banshees chasing them bounced off the clouds.

Tor lay back against stone at a precarious seventy-degree angle. Through gasping breaths, he said, "Iolar Mór Bán can't be worse than that."

19
IOLAR MÓR BÁN

"DON'T hold your breath."

All three teens turned their heads in the direction of the voice with a cawing rasp.

Just above them to their left on a boulder larger than a dozen pop-bubbles, sat a huge onyx bird, bigger than three Yeti.

The bird shook its head. "She is in a tizzy. Might snap your heads right off without proper procedure."

Looks of astonishment on the faces of the humans led to, "Caw! Caw! Caw!" with what sounded strangely like a chuckle. "Have you never seen a talking Raven?"

The three shook their heads.

"Well, now you have. I am Caitheamh Tobar, but you may call me Toby. I saw you on Carrion Tuirlingthe."

"No way," Tor muttered. "The only bird we saw was a raven that landed on Chriostalach's arm. You are by far too big."

"That's right. When I descend to the plain, I grow smaller. "He cocked his head to the side. "You aren't afraid of me."

Tor pointed. "You seem harmless after that."

"Don't you know that my kind portend death? Or at least bad news?"

All three sat up. Terk said, "I don't think you plan to kill us, or you would have done so already."

"True. I don't find human flesh very tasty."

Tor scratched his head. "Chriostalach said she could not help us. But you can. At least now that we've made it this far."

"Quite perceptive. She did not instruct me to assist you, but I've known her a long time. She would prefer to be by your side. Alas, wicket guardians have restrictions." He ruffled his feathers.

"So, I guess we keep climbing," Tor grunted.

"No," Toby said. "I'll take you, but first you must rest. If you are breathing this hard, you might suffocate during the ascent. The air gets very thin up top."

The three looked from one to the other. "I *am* tired," Tae said.

"Then, rest," Toby said. "I'll be right here when you wake up."

"I'm freezing," Terk grumbled.

Tor added, "And hungry."

"Eat," the bird commanded.

Once they had eaten, Toby swooshed to stand beside them. He nestled to the ground and raised a massive wing. His feathers ruffled. "I make a great blanket. Come."

***

A frigid draught woke the teens. Caitheamh Tobar had lifted his wing. "Rise and shine," he said in his gravelly voice. "Time to meet the Queen Mother."

Tor yawned. "So, where's the King?"

The huge bird blinked several times before he answered, "Pearlan."

"Which is where, exactly?" asked Tae.

Toby squawked, "Where you do not want to go at such a young age, but where everyone wants to go someday, where the gods reside."

Terk whispered, "He's dead."

"Yes." The massive black head bobbed.

"How?" asked Tor. "He had to be bigger than you and a lot deadlier himself."

"Ah," Toby rumbled. "He granted audience to Leviaddan."

"Our uncle killed him?" Terk shrieked.

Toby's beak snapped shut. "Uncle?" barely escaped through his breathing holes.

Tor laid a hand on his sister's and mumbled, "Diplomacy." He turned to Toby. "Yes. He has imprisoned our father, and we are seeking to find the enchanted items that can free him."

Tae ventured, "How does the Queen live?"

Toby relaxed. "Leviaddan killed Rí Na H-iolair before they even spoke, but Leviaddan made the mistake of angering a nesting female. I'm certain if you ever get close enough to see him face-to-face, you will witness his scars. Do not anger Iolar Mór Bán. She is already in a dither, but she has not told me why."

He stood and shimmied. Lowering a wing, he said, "Climb onto my back and hold on tightly."

The girls squealed at first, but they quickly acclimated to the thrill. Tor said, "How awesome! This is what Mamere could do—and"—He made a gagging sound—"Leviaddan."

"But not Papere," Tae muttered.

"*Yet*," Terk asserted.

Higher and higher they flew until the air became frosty and bit into exposed skin.

Then, they saw it—Two-miles in diameter, a nest with smaller nests nestled around the perimeter; and at the summit, an eagle in a nest half-a-mile across. So brilliantly white was her plumage that it reflected a blinding prism of color.

Around her flopped three eaglets, gangly and drab.

"If Rí Na H-iolair is dead, how does she have babies?" Tae mused.

"She was nesting," Terk reminded. "The eggs had not hatched."

Toby murmured. "I only see three—Prince Rhagclaw, the heir, is missing."

"Missing?" Tor said.

Caitheamh Tobar landed on the rim of Iolar Mór Bán's nest and dipped his head. "Your Majesty."

The triplets slid to the Raven's feet and bowed.

In a reverberating screech, the Queen screamed, "Kill them!"

20
NEGOTIATION

IOLAR Mór Bán's scream began a rumble beneath the summit as snow cascaded down the mountain.

Caitheamh Tobar covered the triplets with his wing. "Why, Your Majesty?" he asked. "What have they done?"

Peeking through black feathers, the teens saw great tears well in the eyes of the magnificent Eagle.

"I have no choice. Leviaddan's minions have stolen Prince Rhagclaw. He demands their lives as ransom."

Tor slid from Toby's tentative protection and dropped to his knees, head bowed. "Your Majesty, he will not return your son even if you kill us. He is a liar. He is our common enemy. At least, give us the opportunity to rescue Prince Rhagclaw."

"What did he say?" Tae asked Terk.

"He just bought us time—diplomacy."

The Queen Mother stood and shimmied. Her little ones ran to her and hid beneath her wing. "How do you plan to get my son back from a god?"

"Ah!" Tor held up an index finger, head still bowed. "First, Leviaddan is *not* a god."

Iolar Mór Bán leaned forward. "Tell me more, little man."

Tor told the Queen Mother everything Yarwhin had told them. She listened without interruption.

Tor's knees ached, and every sinew was taut.

"Hm," came from Iolar Mór Bán's mouth like a coo. "Can you kill him?"

"Alas, no, Your Majesty. Only my father can kill him, unless you have Nephilim on Örnland. But with your help, we can free my father."

The Queen's feathers rippled. "But you are willing to try to rescue my son in exchange for one of my feathers?"

"Yes."

Iolar Mór Bán lifted her wings, and the three eaglets ventured out, heading directly to Tor and encircling him.

"They trust you," the Queen said. "Very well. There are a few things you must know. It is the season of light, so Mountain Trolls will be no problem. They turn to stone in sunlight. Even mobile, they lumber and are slow, though they have a powerful punch, nearly as deadly as a Yeti's. However, your uncle came here and chose mates among them. Their offspring are abundant, fast, and mean. Ugly creatures too. We call them Orcs. Though not as large as Trolls, they are deadlier, proficient with bow and arrow and battleax. And they are fast and agile."

Tor puffed out a disgusted breath. "He created a warrior race, Danooks, on Salymra when he chose Wulfgar mates. But they were more mindless beasts until recently."

"Orcs are smart, but you cannot negotiate with them. They show no mercy. If Prince Rhagclaw lives, return him to me. If not, bring me his remains and the head of his killer. Then, you may have your feather."

Tor stood. "Where should we begin our search?"

"Trolls live under bridges."

Tor backed away, head still bowed. Once he stepped behind Toby, he stood straight. The Raven nudged him back more with a subtle wing push, and Tae and Terk joined him.

Toby spoke. "Your Majesty, permission to accompany."

"No. They would see you a hundred miles away. But change their furs to blend with the snow."

"Back up with me," Toby muttered. They backed away until they were beyond the Queen's guard. Tor rubbed his knees when they stopped moving.

The Raven turned. "You heard. Let's get you supplied. I'm sure there are more weapons for you too." He pointed his beak toward a cave where the triplets found, not only weapons, but also armor, which Toby insisted they wear.

Outfitted, the triplets stood before Toby. "Good," he said.

"Where do we find bridges?" Tor asked.

"They will be ice," Toby said. "Look for dark areas. The bridges will appear to have a blue tint."

"By the gods!" Terk exclaimed. "This is one time I wish we could fly."

Tor scratched his chin. "This armor is heavy. Perhaps we can float on a cloud." He began to form a shape in the air with his hands. Soon, a cloud large enough to hold them and their supplies appeared just at hip height.

He looked from one sister to the other. "Let's try it."

The three of them sat on the fluffiness. The cloud lowered a bit with their weight. "It's holding," Tor said.

They pulled their feet up, and when Tor gave a large puff of air, the cloud moved. "Pray to the gods for us," Tor said to Toby with a wave.

***

The cloud floated along, and the triplets scanned the surface for ice bridges. Every time they breathed, tiny frozen crystals hung in the air.

"There!" Tae said in a loud whisper, pointing.

With a waving motion of his hands, Tor maneuvered the cloud around the bridge several times.

Beneath, they saw a good number of huge creatures with alabaster skin all huddled together, sound asleep.

Terk said, "Those must be Trolls. But there is no baby Eagle with them and no Orcs."

"They might be formidable awake, but harmless asleep," Tor said. "They are also Leviaddan's victims. I will not harm them."

An hour later, Tae spotted something else. "Movement to your left."

Tor steered their flying cloud toward the movement and hovered.

Below, two dozen black-and-white creatures about seven feet tall drank something that even from their perch above them smelled foul. They were two-toned, just like Leviaddan, though not divided in half, with some checkered, some striped, and some with no pattern. Unlike Danooks, they wore leather thongs to cover their private parts, as had the Trolls.

In a cage an Eaglet with bronze feathers and a golden cap shrieked and ran or flapped its wings to only go a few feet, each time an Orc threw a sharp projectile at it. They would laugh uproariously and slurp more of the putrid beverage.

"Alcohol is fueling their frenzy," Tor said.

"Poor little Rhagclaw," Terk murmured.

Tae set her jaw. "I say we rid Örnland of a few Orcs." She nocked an arrow.

"Agreed." Terk found a flat, sharp stone for her sling.

Tor reached for a javelin. "Once we fire, they'll fight back. Still, I'd rather engage them from here than hand-to-hand."

Tae pulled back her bow string. "Make every shot count and keep them away from the Prince."

"On three," Tor said and counted.

Simultaneously, the triplets released their shots, felling three Orcs.

Closing ranks, the other Orcs looked around to find where the assault originated. The teens hunkered into the cloud for cover as they readied another barrage.

Three more Orcs fell, ebony blood staining the pearly, pristine snow.

Rhagclaw screamed as some of the blood splattered him, drawing attention to himself.

An Orc started for the cage. Tae's arrow entered his temple. He slumped onto the enclosure, causing it to sway and groan under his weight.

The Eagle Prince screeched and ran around in circles.

Terk and Tor got off another shot, leaving fifteen enemies standing.

Tor pointed to one Orc apart from the others. "Female with a suckling infant."

She held the child close and cowered against the side of the bridge.

"Protecting her babe," Terk said. "It's what a mother does."

A roar accompanied a flying battleax.

With screams of their own, the triplets hurtled to the ground as the cloud split. Each pulled their short-range weapons.

The Orcs charged toward them, axes flailing. Battling not only foes, but also the alien weight of armor, Tor managed to block a downward strike with his sword and thrust his hidden dagger into an Orc's chest.

Terk taunted three Orcs into following her. Spinning with her two short swords, she cut each one across their middle, their innards spilling onto the ground. Her armor shielded her from a blow that would have been fatal.

Despite the extra weight, Tae battled two Orcs at once, fleetly kicking, parrying, and finding their throats.

At last, only the largest male, the female, and the child remained.

"Flank the woman," Tor said.

"You aren't going to kill a baby!" Terk yelled.

"Just listen."

Tae nocked an arrow and aimed. Terk loaded her sling and began to spin, but she begged, "Please, Tor."

"Trust me. I have a theory. Notice he's the biggest. He fought each of us, moving from one to the other. He's the alpha, band leader." He raised a javelin.

With a roar that shook the ground and echoed through the vale, the male charged to stand in front of the female, battleax across his chest, violent snorts emanating from his throat.

Terk gasped. "And *that* is what a father should do."

"Exactly," said Tor. "Now, if I can figure out Orc diplomacy."

He pointed at the female and child. "Them for him." He pointed at Prince Rhagclaw.

The Orc snorted and backed up closer to the female.

Tor pointed to the dead Orcs. "Leviaddan's fault."

"Lev-Lev."

"Yes," Tor said. "He doesn't care for you. You are his pawns in a crazy game." He touched his chest. "Tor." And then he pointed at Tae and Terk and said their names.

Still in attack stance, the Orc thumped his ax against his chest. "Veelar." He gave a quick look over his shoulder. "Neeshawn."

The female looked up.

The Orc spoke again. "Creenon." He lifted his ax. "Lev-Lev." He drew the ax across his abdomen, bringing a thin line of blood.

"No," Tor said. "Take your family and go to the Yetis."

"Yeti? No Lev-Lev?"

"That's right," Terk said, "The Yetis rejected him and hid."

A sound like stampeding cattle drew all their attention. Another band of Orcs stopped just beyond the bodies. Veelar stepped forward and roared. The largest member of the other band came forward. Axes clashed.

"No!" Tor yelled. With a blast of energy, he sent an arc of chain lightning that electrified the entire attacking band, traveling from one to the other with a loud buzzing.

Veelar turned toward Tor, ax at his side. He pointed toward the second band. "Fight. Always." He drew circles in the air.

"Your bands always fight among themselves?" Tor asked.

"Always."

"Take your family. Go to the Yetis. Ask for Goliab."

Veelar pointed to the cage. "Take."

Holding out his hand and grunting, Neeshawn ran to him. They left at a fast trot.

Tor approached the cage. Rhagclaw ran to the farthest corner. "Blankets," Tor said to his sisters. He held out his hand to the Eaglet. "It's okay. We came to take you home."

Rhagclaw screeched a shrill, "Ma-ma-ma."

"Yes," Tor said. "To your mother."

Terk handed him a blanket.

"Come," Tor said, holding out the comforting cloth.

Timidly, the young Prince inched toward Tor. When he reached him, Tor wrapped Rhagclaw snuggly in the blanket.

Though young, the giant Eaglet already weighed fifty pounds.

"Feel up to making another cloud?" Terk asked.

"No need!" Tae pointed.

A big black bird flew toward them.

"He disobeyed the Queen!" Tor said in disbelief.

21
A POUND IS A POUND

TOBY landed just beyond the bloodied battleground.

"By the gods!" Tor shouted. "The Queen forbade you to come with us."

"I did *not* come with you. I only came when I saw the second band of Orcs. Then, I saw two Orcs running down the mountain." He ruffled his feathers. "Still, perhaps, this should be our secret."

"I agree," Tor said, looking down at the bundle he held. Prince Rhagclaw was sound asleep.

"Come," Toby said. "I'll leave you a day's journey out, past the Banshees.

"Thank the gods," Terk said. "One battle with them was enough."

Toby asked, "Do you still have food?"

"Enough," Tae said, climbing onto Toby's back. She helped her sister up, who reached down and took the sleeping Prince. Then, Tor joined them after passing packs.

"Shouldn't we do something about the bodies?" Terk asked.

"No," Toby said. "The carrion eaters need food too."

At the, "Yuck!" he turned his head.

"It is the way of life. Now, did you find the container with the gooey stuff?"

"Yes," Tor said. "What is that? It tasted foul, but we kept it."

Toby chuckled. "I had faith in you. It's for Prince Rhagclaw when he wakes. There is a scoop in Terk's pack to feed him."

Terk puffed out her cheeks. "Will he snap my hand off?"

"No," Toby assured. "You are Terra-Firma Elemental."

"He's too young to understand that," she argued.

"He'll sense it well enough. Now, burrow beneath my feather so that you won't blow off. "

They flew along in relative silence after that. Toby chuckled once he heard the distinct sound of four snores.

***

A soft thud woke the triplets. Toby said, "I leave you here. The rest of your journey should be easy."

They slid from the Raven's back. Prince Rhagclaw began to stir.

Toby said, "Make camp. Eat. Rest some more, and come back tomorrow." He soared away.

The Eagle Prince began to scream, "Ma-ma-ma!"

Terk soothed, "Sh. I bet you're hungry."

Tae found the food for the Eaglet, and Terk offered him a bite. He dipped his beak at it and then opened his mouth wide, gobbling half the container.

"Do you burp Eaglets?" Terk asked.

"No clue," her siblings chorused.

Rhagclaw wiggled furiously. Terk let him loose. He ran behind the nearest tree but was soon back to his rescuers. "He had to relieve himself," she mumbled.

"Me too," Tor said and started toward the tree line.

A terrified screech from the Prince made him turn around.

Veelar and Neeshawn approached at a high lope. They stopped short of the teens. Veelar looked over his shoulder.

"We flew," Tor said to the questioning on the Orc's face, and he made wing-flapping motions with his hands. "Relax. Take a deep breath."

Veelar covered his ears. Tor turned to Terk. "Calm Rhagclaw down."

She lifted the bird and turned her back to the Orcs as she whispered assurance to the young Prince.

The triplets made camp, and Tor indicated for Veelar and Neeshawn to join them.

Rhagclaw finally stopped screaming but stayed at Terk's feet as far away from the two Orcs as he could get. But when Creenon began to cry, Rhagclaw peeked around Terk's legs.

"It's another child," Terk said. "Can Creenon sit without help?"

Neeshawn looked up at her mate. He nodded. She put the baby on the ground.

Rhagclaw dashed out, touched Creenon with his beak, and ran back.

Creenon laughed.

Seven times, the Eaglet did this. The last time, Creenon reached out and touched him. Then, it seemed as if the two children carried on a conversation that nobody understood.

As the little ones jabbered, the others talked. Veelar's vocabulary was limited, so he augmented by drawing pictures in the snow.

The triplets soon discovered that his band had not taken Rhagclaw. They had snatched him from the band that came after them. Veelar wanted to return him, but he did not know what to do and feared the Queen's wrath.

Before they all slept, it was decided that Veelar and his family would stay with Goliab. Tor would relay the information to Iolar Mór Bán.

***

After they awoke and breakfasted, they all walked into the forest.

Terk called loudly, "Goliab!"

Before long, the mammoth Yeti appeared without menace.

Terk told him the whole story. He beckoned the Orc family to follow him. They all disappeared into the woods.

Tor shouldered his pack. "Prince?" he said.

The Eaglet bounced up and down at his feet. Tor laughed. "All right. Walk. Let us know if you get tired."

As they tramped through the forest, Rhagclaw explored, always only a few feet away. When they came to a stream, he splashed among the floes and returned with his own fish.

"I'm hungry, too," Tor said.

The meal finished, they continued their journey, but Rhagclaw slowed. Tor scooped him up. "You're tired." The Eaglet gave a little squeak and laid his head on Tor's shoulder.

"He'll get heavy," Tae warned.

"I'll hand him off." He grinned. "We'll take turns."

Near the tree line, that would yield a wide-open area, they made camp. Rhagclaw hopped up and down, seeing the wide expanse. "Ma-ma-ma!"

"Tomorrow," Tor said. "We need to rest."

Without argument, the Prince snuggled next to Tor and went to sleep again.

***

"Ma-ma-ma!" woke the triplets.

They stared out across the blue-white span. Indeed, in the distance, they saw Iolar Mór Bán and Toby flying toward them. They packed up camp as fast as they could.

Not long later, the two massive birds landed. Rhagclaw raced to his mother, wings flapping and giving him a few yards of flying. The teens bowed.

"Your Majesty," Tor began.

"Give me a report. Who took my son?"

Tor told her all he knew, even about the Orcs fleeing Leviaddan's control.

"So? Am I supposed to welcome this Veelar and his family?" Iolar Mór Bán asked.

"I would hope so," Tor said. "If there are more with his mindset, they could be allies once my father is free."

"I suppose we might be allies. We do have a common enemy." She chuckled. "Tell me, young Tor—Which will fall faster, a pound of rocks or a pound of feathers?"

"I would think a pound is a pound." He held up his finger. "Unless the wind somehow manages to blow the feathers if they are not tightly packed."

"Interesting, *if.*" She scratched her chest with her talons and pulled a huge plume loose. "We had an agreement." She held out the feather.

Tor took it and held it to his side. It rustled above his head as a breeze blew.

The Queen continued, "Guard Quill well. You might find she holds some powerful magic." She turned to her companion. "Caitheahm Tobar will take you back to the wicket now. When Yarwhin is free, contact Örnland. We will fight by his side."

With Rhagclaw snug beneath her back feathers, Iolar Mór Bán flew away.

22
QUILL

CHRIOSTALACH met Toby and the triplets at the wicket. Once the teens dismounted, the Raven shrank back to the size of a large bird and sat on the Elf's arm.

She handed Tor a crystal orb that twinkled gray, white, and blue. Giving the teens a bow, she said, "When you need to return to Örnland, bring this with you. It will grant you passage, unhindered. Once through the wicket, you can speak to it, and it will take you wherever you tell it."

Tor gave her a bow, and his sisters curtsied. They touched Toby's head. "Thank you," Tor said.

The Raven, now in a voice that sounded like a child's, said, "I count it an honor to call you friends."

The wicket began to swirl. "Salmyra," Chriostalach spoke with command. To the triplets she said, "Remember, all at once." Then, she stared toward the horizon. "We must hurry home. Darkness is upon us. Remember if you return during the dark season, do not dally. Evil and danger lurk in the night."

The teens clasped hands and leapt through the wicket.

Tor laughed when they came out on the mountaintop. "I guess we have a long walk."

Quill shuddered. Tor let go of his grip on the plume, and it laid itself in a prone position.

Terk said, "Quill is offering us a ride."

"By the gods!" Tor exclaimed.

Tae said, "Iolar Mór Bán said Quill has powerful magic."

They floated silently along, as if on a bed of the softest cotton. Coming upon the valley where the Danooks had been slaughtered, they saw sun-bleached bones.

Tor mumbled, "How long were we gone?"

"I don't know," Tae whispered.

Terk followed up, "A long time." She put a hand on her brother's cheek. "You have a full beard, and your hair has grown six inches."

"I can't grow"—Tor touched his own face—"Months? Years?" He looked from sister to sister.

Terk sighed. "At least six months. Six, woman cycles. And Chriostalach said darkness was upon them."

"Why does time seem so different when we're away?" Tor asked.

Tae said, "Because each world has a different rotation and revolution of their sun. Terk is right, and our cycles could have adjusted to Örnland time. Let's just get home."

***

Seeing the hedge Terk had put in place did not ease their minds. She whispered, "I have seen no travelers. And my hedge is almost crisp from lack of rain."

"Do you think Leviaddan put an even worse drought on the area?" Tae asked.

"Maybe," Tor responded, "in retaliation."

"What if Mamere had to leave?" Tae asked with a catch in her voice.

"Then she'll have left a message." Tor gave his sister a smile.

At the hedge, they dismounted Quill, and the feather came to Tor's side.

They carefully picked their way through the brambles meant to be protection to the secret entrance.

Pausing at the door that looked like tangled vines, now wilted, Tor listened. "I hear nothing."

Terk waved him on, but both she and Tae pulled daggers.

Tor pushed the door open.

Two lances greeted his neck.

In a voice an octave lower than when he left, "Mamere?" he asked, not being able to see in the darkness within.

"Tor!" a child's voice shouted. From the shadows, raced a little boy Tor hardly recognized.

"Iontus!" Tor said, doubting his senses. He picked up the child on the side away from Quill.

Illuminet and Fuascailt pulled back their lances.

"Thank the gods!" Illuminet exclaimed. "You're finally home." She turned to Fauscailt. "Light a tallow, but just one."

"What's going on?" Tor asked.

Illuminet lifted her hands as if in surrender. "This past year has been unbelievable. Daily raids by humans in the daylight and by Danooks at night. It's only rained twice. We've dug a well, but it's low."

"And now," Fuascailt added, "the condors carry off living beings. Venturing out for food is perilous." She stole glances at Tor when she returned with the lit tallow.

"A year?" he said. He put Iontus down and held his arm out to Fuascailt. She went to him, putting her arms around his waist. He pulled her close, and his chin brushed the top of her head.

She lifted a hand to his face. "You have more hair than me now. And you're so tall."

Illuminet stared at the large feather at Tor's side.

"Meet Quill," he said. The plume gave a bow and Tor introduced everyone.

Sudden howls got their attention. Illuminet barred the door. "All other entrances stay barricaded," she said.

"We need to get Quill to Papere as soon as possible," Tor said.

Illuminet said, "You can leave in the morning."

"This time, you're going with us." He looked at his mother and sweetheart. "All of you."

Illuminet started to speak. Tor gently touched his mother's lips with a finger. "Don't argue."

***

"Wake up, wake up!" Iontus trilled, shaking Tor.

"Oh," Tor groaned. "One day to sleep would be so nice."

"Grandmere has breakfast." The little boy pulled Tor's hand. "She's using honey in the pottage today."

Tor followed Iontus. Everyone else was already there. He saw that each person had a small bowl, and Illuminet opened the honey. Iontus clapped.

Tor frowned. "Mamere, what have you been eating?"

"Food has been scarce," Illuminet said. "Let's enjoy what we have."

"Yes, Mamere," He patted his mother's hand. "Then we need to go."

Illuminet formed a thin line with her lips.

"You're going," Tor said firmly.

The meal finished, they packed the last bit of food they had and a few garments. They filled water skins from the well and started out.

Tor secured Quill to his side with a belt.

"Where do we go?" Illuminet asked once they were outside.

In the light, Tor saw two curved blades on Fuascailt's belt. She followed his gaze. "I'm very good with these."

Tor took her hand. "Let's hope we don't have to use them." He turned to Iontus. "Little man, want to ride on my back?"

"Yes!" Iontus raised his arms to be picked up.

"Tor," Fuascailt said, "he'll get heavy."

"We'll take turns carrying him. He can't keep up, and we need to move fast."

"Where are we going?" Illuminet asked again.

"The place where we fell through to Papere," Tor replied.

They moved at a fast clip all day, eating on the move, taking quick swigs of water. Several times, they skirted groups of travelers, Fuascailt being careful to keep a scarf over her face.

They made it to Yggamay and once again slept in her branches. Howling and clashing weapons made for restless repose.

The pace through the forest was slower, and they got to the passage through Danook outcroppings near dusk.

The sound of many feet running behind them spurred them on.

"No Danooks are reaching for us," Tae said.

Fuascailt informed, "This area has been raided many times."

Pounding footsteps from the other direction made them stop.

Giant wing-flapping above caused them to look up.

"By the gods!" Tor exclaimed.

"Traitor!" Leviaddan roared. "You will pay!" He reached down and grabbed Fuascailt's arm.

"Let her go!" Tor yelled.

"What can you do?" Leviaddan snarled. "You're mere flesh and blood."

Tor pulled his sword. Quill loosened and hopped to the others.

Tor, swinging his sword with all his might, nearly severed his uncle's hand from his arm.

Leviaddan's cry shook the earth. Stones began to roll down the sides of the canyon.

"We're trapped!" Illuminet shrieked.

"No!" Fuascailt grabbed Tor's hand. "This way. Just run!"

They followed her into a tunnel. A quarter mile of running with stampeding marauders on their heels, they came to a cavern.

"It's a Danook den," Fuascailt said through gasps.

A raider with raised hammer charged toward her.

"No!" Tor bellowed, swinging his sword, downing the attacker.

"We can't fight all of them!" Illuminet cried. "And Leviaddan!"

Terk lifted her hands, palms up, and pulled down.

Rocks and dirt filled the tunnel, blocking them in the cavern in total darkness.

"What now?" Tor asked. "We're trapped in here."

Illmuminet managed a small orb of light in her palm.

Quill began to wiggle side-to-side.

"Okay," Tor said. "What do you have in mind?"

Quill folded in half and then shot her shaft into the ground. Then, she began to spin, faster and faster, her barbs slapping, a whirlwind forming around her. "Grab hold!" echoed from the swirl.

Everyone latched on to a barb.

A jolt.

A moment of freefalling.

BAM!

A hard landing on cold stone.

23
A GIFT FOR MAMERE

FAST-MOVING light coming toward them made the Salmyrans regain their composure and arm themselves.

"Yarwhin!" Iluminet cried, dropping her weapon and racing to the figure that appeared.

Yarwhin let the Fire Brazier of Lavan clatter to the stone. "Illuminet!" He gathered her to him and smothered her with kisses.

The rest of them rose. Yarwhin released Illuminet and held out his arms to his children, hugging each in turn. "Are you all right?" He finally asked and turned his gaze to Fuascailt with Iontus hiding behind her and the giant feather that bounced up and down beside her. "I believe introductions are in order."

Tor returned to stand beside those who held back. "Papere, let me present Quill, your staunch ally sent by Iolar Mór Bán."

Quill gave a bow.

"My!" Yarwhin exclaimed. "I had no idea you would be—alive. Thank you for coming."

Tor continued. "Papere, this is Fuascailt and her son, Iontus."

Yarwhin cocked an eyebrow.

Fuascailt moved closer to Tor.

"Let me guess," Yarwhin said, "Leviaddan's creations."

"Yes, Papere," Tor said. "But she is *not* with him." He took her hand. "She's for me, and I will raise Iontus as my own."

Yarwhin turned to Illuminet for explanation.

"It's true," she said.

"Uncle," Fuascailt found her voice. "I am a victim, just as you are. I offer you my allegiance and assistance." She took a deep breath. "I am not a spy for my father. Why would I be, considering?" She glanced down at her son. "No. I am for Tor as Aunt Illuminet is for you. I know it was not my father's intent, but his plan is not to be."

Yarwhin folded his arms across his chest. "Tor, you have found a strong woman." He dropped his arms to his sides. "Welcome, Fuascailt and Iontus." He held out his arms.

Tor nudged Fuascailt, and she went forward, towing her son. Yarwhin hugged his niece and knelt to be closer to the child. "Little one, you have many features from your grandmother, Fayla. I vow to keep you safe. May I have a hug?"

Iontus let go of his mother's hand and put his arms around Yarwhin's neck. At the contact, Yarwhin began to gasp, and a myriad of pictures flooded his mind. He held the child at arms' length. "You have a great gift."

"What do you mean, Grandpere?"

"Grandpere?"

"He calls me Grandmere," Illuminet said. "So, it's logical for you to be Grandpere."

Yarwhin nodded. "Yes, it is. Iontus, you showed me things when we hugged. I need to process the images, but you might be a huge help in my children's quests." He placed a kiss on the little boy's forehead.

"He already has been," Illuminet said and told Yarwhin about the scrolls.

"Hm. And the obsidian did not hamper his abilities." Yarwhin rolled his lips. "Now," he said with a wrinkled nose, "I think everyone could use a bath while I order us some food. Then, I want to hear *all* about what happened."

As if one, the young people sniffed an armpit, causing Yarwhin to chortle.

***

Washed and refreshed, they sat down to venison stew and barley loaves. There was a bowl of honey, which caused Iontus to dance around in anticipation. Yarwhin smiled at the child's delight, but his heart ached that such a small delicacy could cause so much joy.

Yarwhin asked, "Quill, do you require nourishment?"

In answer, the plume dipped itself in a pitcher of water. An unnoticed droop turned to a perky stance of the feather's blades.

"I shall be sure you have plenty of water," Yarwhin declared.

As they ate, the triplets told Yarwhin about their quest and the allies they had made, as well as known enemies.

"You have done well, Tor." He took Illuminet's hand. "And now, Terk must prepare." He looked toward Iontus. "However, you can't go back to Libretante."

"But all the scrolls are there," Terk said, her face blanching. "Even with all we read, Tor faced many unknowns. I need to prepare."

"But not at Libretante. Leviaddan has found it." Yarwhin set his jaw firmly.

Terk stretched her eyes wide. "Then where? Here?"

"Let's discuss it later. Quill has something to share." Yarwhin nodded toward the feather.

The large plume dipped her top at the acknowledgement. She hopped to stand beside Illuminet. Shaking with force, two of her barbules fell to the floor. She dipped her top several times from Illuminet to the pieces of down.

"Pick them up, Mamere," Tor said, his mind running wild.

Illuminet picked up the two pieces of down large enough to be a normal feather from a big bird.

Quill lifted into the air and floated back down.

Illuminet blinked, understanding, not understanding, daring to hope.

Iontus ran his fingers across Quill and then put his hand on Illuminet's cheek. He whispered, "A gift, Grandmere. Quill says to put them where your wings used to be, and they will grow back."

Illuminet burst into tears.

24
ONE STEP CLOSER

"I never dreamed...It's too good..." Illuminet sobbed.

Yarwhin held her to him. "My love, my Angel, your sacrifice has been rewarded." He held her face in his hands and kissed her tears away. "Give me the down."

Illuminet handed the soft feathers to him.

He gently slipped her blouse over her shoulders and down her back. She kept it tightly clasped in front.

Yarwhin glanced at Quill. "Is there any particular way to lay them?"

Quill shimmied back and forth.

With the shaft pointing down, Yarwhin carefully placed the feather along Illuminet's jagged scars. The skin made a soft sucking sound, and the plumes held fast.

Iontus spoke again. "Quill says it will take time. They will grow." He looked up at the giant feather with his brow furrowed. "I don't understand those words.

Quill's blades ruffled up and down.

"Oh." The little boy nodded. "When they are full-grown, you will be able to open them and fly, but you can close them, and they will become a cloak. Your clothes will need to have slits for them."

"I understand," Illuminet said, still in shock. "How can I ever thank you?"

Iontus puckered his lips. "Beat Leviaddan."

Yarwhin chuckled. "That is our goal, but now, we must turn our attention to Terk."

Terk said, "If we can't go back to the scrolls, how can I study and learn?"

Yarwhin placed a hand on Iontus's head. "This child has a great gift. His touch showed me many things."

He looked from Iontus to Fuascailt. "The two of you will need to stay here with me." He jutted his chin. "In the other room, just in case Leviaddan looks for you."

"Tor!" Fuascailt's voice caught.

Tor took her hand. "It'll be fine."

Yarwhin looked toward the overhang. "I know where to send you. Illuminet will go with you, but she cannot go on the quest with you. Iontus showed me caves with markings. I believe they are in Reoite Tundra Theas," He studied the triplets' faces. "Melita's land."

No one spoke for a long time. Terk finally asked, "When do we leave?"

Yarwhin smiled. "I'm selfish enough to want one day with my family. Tomorrow." He went to the overhang. "Parchment, quill, and ink."

The items appeared. He turned back, "I'll send a letter of introduction with you. I'll be waiting for your return."

32,263 words
9/3/2018

ABOUT THE AUTHOR

LIKE many of her characters, Janet is a history buff and loves anything of historical significance from old cars to old cemeteries. Get to know Janet and you'll see why she's been critically acclaimed at the Faulkner Wisdom Competition and why her writing continues to receive 4 and 5-star reviews, as well as winning awards—It could be that readers see so much of her in her characters: mother, educator, author, editor, native Mississippian, graduate of the University of Southern Mississippi and Belhaven University, and a person who has overcome great obstacles and still holds on to her faith.

http://www.janettaylorperry.com/
http://janettaylor-perry.blogspot.com/
https://authorcentral.amazon.com/gp/profile
https://www.facebook.com/Author-Janet-Taylor-Perry-299698950061301/
janettaylorperry@gmail.com
https://www.facebook.com/janettaylorperrybooks/
Instagram: @janettaylorperry & @jtaylorperry
Twitter: Janet Taylor-Perry— @mom5kidz421
Goodreads:
https://www.goodreads.com/author/show/7376480.Janet_Taylor_Perry
Pinterest: https://www.pinterest.com/mumzy25/
YouTube: https://bit.ly/30hJsYg

THE IGNIS TRIPLETS RETURN IN BOOK 2 OF *GODS AND CHILDREN*

Ain't No Valley

TOR'S quest is finished! But Yarwhin still needs two more mystical artifacts to escape his obsidian prison.

In Book 2 of the *God's and Children* series, the Ignis triplets continue their search for the items to free their father.

Terk is Terra-Firma Elemental. It's now her turn to go on a mission. Of course, the triplets understand that the three of them must work together to accomplish their goals. Terk's journey takes them to, yet, another world where she meets a horribly disfigured Elven Prince who steals her heart and joins her in a dangerous trek to the Marbled Mines where they hope to find The Goblet of Godetta, the Dragon Goddess.

They encounter enchanted and deadly plants, Were-animals, testy Dwarves, Ogres, and more in their quest. Terk learns just how powerful her ability to heal is, making her even more valuable to Yarwhin's cause.

But does she have the power to restore the dead? Whom will they lose on this trip?